I'M SLEEPING

MATTHEW FIST

THE PAPER HOUSE
PUBLISHING

Disclaimer:

This book is based on a true story. Names, Descriptions, Places, and Locations have been changed.

Trigger Warnings:

This book contains: Drug and Alcohol use, Mental Illness/Bipolar Hypersexuality, Sexual Acts, Edging, Sadism, Degradation, Gaslighting, Cheating, Reverse Harem

CONTENTS

PREFACE

What happened could never be fixed or forgiven, and I understand why Mel never confessed anything to me. But she never wanted anything to be fixed or forgiven. The fact that I loved and desired her played right into her sadistic mind. She enjoyed using me, then rejecting me while maintaining her secret life and would say anything to keep it going. My sexual angst turned her on. The more frustrated I got, the more she enjoyed it. I didn't understand what she was doing and pushed her to open up more, and she did, just not with me. I was unknowingly contributing to her hypersexual mania.

I recently read a memoir documenting the destructive nature of bipolar hypersexuality. But it was written by the villain after she was exposed. To me, it's just chasing a high, a taboo high. I suppose it's relative to the individual. Imagine a scale from one to ten. One being very conservative or vanilla thoughts and ten possibly being a devil's threesome while your unknowing husband sleeps in the other room. Mel treated me as level one or two, and I wanted level five or six, whatever that may be. Mel secretly lived at level ten, and because of what her dad told me, I believe Mel had these issues since she was a child. But sex was only half of it. The other half needed to torture someone.

Mental illness is society's way of explaining and labeling unacceptable or abnormal behavior, which seems to be increasing. It's a time of instant gratification, and with instant highs, you also get lows. Everyone chases a high and the rush of endorphins that come with it. It is human nature, and no one is immune. Chase what makes you happy. The problem is when people make bad decisions and blame mental illness. Society tries to force everyone to accept their behavior based on a medical diagnosis. I'm not saying I have any answers, only observations in my case. I'm just an engineer.

I'm also not a writer. But this is my story, and I put it together differently. It is a timeline of events, as the table of contents displays. At the end of chapters three through nine, I downloaded, edited, and inserted our texts during those periods. It was my intention for you to better understand how hard it was to distinguish reality and I think it hits harder than typing in he-said/she-said content. You can see the level of gaslighting for yourself. Notice that Mel acknowledged very little and avoided texting anything incriminating. It seems she's been down this road before and always stayed ahead of me.

Initially, I researched defamation laws, and know I have to change more things, but I continued writing, and near the end, I learned about including texts in a book. It seems texts are copywrite protected and cannot be published. Nice. Well, I guess the only person to see my original memoir will be an editor or writing coach. Hopefully, we can put something good together.

ONE
THE BEGINNING (2011 - 2014)

I'VE HEARD before that bad things come in three's but never paid much attention. Meeting Melanie was the third. We met at the office on a Wednesday in August of 2011, but the story started a couple of weeks before. I missed work on Monday and Tuesday that week because I flash-burned half my face by trying to start a bonfire with gasoline while drunk over the weekend. My neighbor friends dragged me to a bar that Saturday night, and I had a few too many. It was probably fate as they told me not to touch the girl I brought home. I was lucky, and the burn was superficial, but that was the only luck I had that night. Probably for the best. I was more embarrassed than anything else. The weekend before, I wrecked on my dirt bike, breaking some bones in my foot. Just some laps around the yard, and I made the mistake of not putting my riding boots on. Oh well, live and learn. I sold the bike not long afterward. That weekend, my roommate brought home two girls from the bar, and one of them stayed with me. It was a fun one-night-er.

So after the first two bad things, I got to the office on Wednesday of that week and limped to my cube. I noticed a new cute girl sitting in an office maybe thirty feet away from me. We locked eyes briefly, and I knew I was in trouble. I forgot that Gary's daughter was starting on Monday that week, and I remembered seeing a pic of her in his cube and thought she was cute. Gary is an older guy in another department, but I occasionally worked with him. He was easy to talk to and knew his job, so I liked him. Although, he was one of those older married guys who always hit on the younger salesgirls that came in. I lose some respect for those types of guys.

Mel noticed me come in, and since I started late that week, I thought everyone had already made introductions. I figured I better hobble into her office and introduce myself. I did, and it turns out that no one else had the nerve—typical bunch of nerds. I worked in engineering, so I guess that's not surprising. I admit I was nervous, though. I knew when our eyes met earlier, so I didn't want to mess it up. Visually Mel had a librarian look with typical office attire. The first thing I noticed was her pretty eyes, which were stripping me of my clothes from the moment she saw me. With a cute face, shoulder-length dark hair on top of a small frame with nice curves, and large natural boobs, I was doing the same with her. As we talked, she said she went by Mel and was thirty-three, divorced twice with no kids, and I told her I was thirty-eight, divorced once with three kids. My burn and limping were obvious, so I explained my stupidity. Then she showed me her tiny hands, which like my burn, I think she wanted to disclose that before I noticed. They were hardly noticeable, and I didn't care. On the plus side, they would make my junk look good, and I told her that. We laughed. We clicked immediately, and all the butterflies of starting something new filled me.

Mel began to take care of me because of my half-burnt face. She would stop by my cube and drop off creams, lotions, and caring application notes. Luckily the burn wasn't bad, just superficial. Mel later admitted that she asked her dad if I went tanning, and he told her, "The dumbass burnt himself." We laughed about it. Soon after, we went out for a date. Everything seemed great. It was already evident that her dad helped her get a job at our company, but I learned he also helped her move back from another state where she spent the last ten years. Mel told me she was an instructor at her old job and was accused of inappropriate behavior with a young intern. She denied it and had a story about how walking away from everything was the best thing to do. That was a red flag that I dismissed. Besides that, she seemed like a cute ordinary girl who was as into me as I was her.

After a couple of weeks of working with each other, the small talk, flirty comments, and looks that could rip your clothes off, things were going to burst. Then Mel invited me over to her apartment. I could not wait, and we attacked each other as soon as I entered her apartment. It was hot initially, but she was reserved and quiet, which was a turn-off for me. We didn't click in bed. Something didn't feel right, and I broke up with her shortly after. Mel was understandably upset, and since we worked together and had to see each other every day, it was tough. I remember my boss telling me not to shit where I eat. Haha, if only. It was a difficult time, and after a couple of weeks, I caved and decided to give us another try. Maybe things in the bedroom would get better.

It went well for a few years, but we always struggled with our sex life. One day I asked Mel if she liked women and if she's ever been with one. She said not sexually but had taken some pictures a long time ago with her brother's girlfriend. She showed me and was proud of them. I thought it was a little weird but also hot. I asked who took the pictures, and she told me some guy that they both knew who had camera equipment. The setting and background looked like a small studio, so ok. The pictures were of them topless with just underwear, touching and holding each other, and some kissing. Mel had some complete nudes by herself. Nothing hardcore, but it was still hot. Another red flag, I suppose.

During the first couple of years, Mel stayed in her apartment, and we would take turns staying with each other. I was renting a home on a few acres with a good amount of wildlife. It was in the suburbs and close to my kids, but no hunting was allowed, and I am a hunter. I took Mel hunting with me a few times. We belly crawled through some thickets, and I even literally pushed her ass thirty feet up a tree. I thought she was a keeper after that. She had never hunted before but told me I reminded her of her grandfather being an outdoorsman and hunter. Her dad also hunted when he was younger but stopped for whatever reason. I rented the house for five years, and in early 2012 the landlord told me I had until the summer. He also owned the property next door and was planning on tearing both houses down and building a dozen homes down a cul-de-sac. So, we began looking for a new home. At the time, Mel's uncle was a real estate agent, so she reached out and asked him to help. He did, and we found the farm I eventually bought. Besides being within a forty-five-minute travel time to my work and obviously within budget, my requirements were: 1) excellent property, 2) pole barn, and 3) some type of mortgageable home. And that is what I got. When Mel, myself, and her uncle first looked at it, we walked past the old house and checked out the barns. They were in disrepair but were worth saving. Then as we walked along the property line, we saw a group of deer on the neighbors' property. The deer saw us coming up the tree line, and instead of running away from us, they crossed our path in front of us to get onto this property. I knew then it was going to be good. It had been vacant for a few years, so everything was overgrown.

The property was awesome and packed full of wildlife—forty acres of mostly hardwoods and a pond. The home was terrible, built in the early 1900s, and not the large style farmhouse.

It was more like a farm hands' house, with seven-foot ceilings, sloping floors built on logs and rocks, and the musty smell to go with it. It needed new everything from foundation to roof. I did what I could with it, and eventually, Mel moved in with me. I had friends and family come by to help work on some projects (barn work, building hunting blinds, planting trees) or to hunt, and they would typically stay the night because it was an hour or more drive for most of them.

We continued our great and busy life, started a garden, did landscaping work, and took a couple of vacations, but we still struggled with our sex life. Mel always went to bed early, like 8-9 p.m., and rejected me ninety percent of the time. It was frustrating because, other than our nightlife, we got along great. Ultimately though, we mutually ended it. She got an apartment, and I helped her move. After the move was over, I didn't communicate with her.

I dated a couple of times, but nothing clicked. I spent the year keeping myself busy on the farm. I didn't know at the time because I never looked back, but I heard Mel ended up with someone else almost immediately, and he moved in with her. His name was Todd, and they met at work. I think he started the day I left that company. A few months later, Todd bought a home, and Mel left her lease early and moved in with him. A couple of months later, Mel picked up her deer mount from the taxidermist. It was her first deer, and she shot it while hunting with me. I video recorded the hunt. A buck appeared around thirty yards out, and she decided that would be the one. I talked her through the motions, and when she squeezed the trigger, the buck dropped instantly. Perfect shot! She was super excited and could hardly speak. She was eager to field dress it and learn.

Anyway, Mel contacted me to show me pics of the finished mount. Not long after, I sent her a happy birthday text just after midnight on her birthday. From what she said, Todd was furious about it. She reached out to me, so something must not be going right. Mel continued to reach out to me several times over the next six months, but purely platonic. Until she told me he was physically abusive to her. I told her I still cared for her and needed to escape that situation. Mel confessed she still cared for me and wanted to see me and check out the farm. We arranged a day, and she came over for a quick visit. We walked down the trail to the pond and talked about things, nothing more. She had lost weight and was about one hundred and fifteen pounds. She looked unhealthy and burned out. I figured toxic Todd was to blame. I never lost my feelings for her, and she wanted to see if she felt the same. A few days later, Mel called me and was crying and said Todd threw her out. I told her she could stay with me but should sleep in the spare bedroom or on the couch. She accepted but never took the spare bed or sofa.

TWO

ROUND TWO (FEB 2015 - AUGUST 2019)

I REMEMBER Mel's first night back, and while we were lying in bed, Todd called me. She said he was abusive, and they just broke up, so I didn't want to talk to him. I didn't answer, but he left a short voice mail. I listened to it afterward, and there were no threats, just some ramblings, so I deleted it. I didn't care. You know what they say, "if you love them, set them free, and if they come back, it's meant to be." A few of my friends seemed concerned, which could be expected because they also say, "They're an ex for a reason." But I was happy, and everything felt right. I knew Mel just went through some shit, so I told her I would not pressure her for sex. To my surprise, she wanted some that night, almost demanded it actually, but vanilla as always. I was ok with it because sex isn't everything, and Mel and I always got along great. We could talk for hours, and we rarely argued, which was nice. We always said good morning and good night with kisses, no matter what our mood was. We always sent good morning and afternoon "I love you" texts during the week, and when I came home from work, I would walk in and say, "family, I'm home!" I think it was more for playtime with the dog than anything else, but it became routine. Whenever the weather was decent, we would take the dog for a hike to the pond and feed the fish.

Often in the evenings, we would watch a movie or show and have popcorn time. Life was great, but there were a couple of red flags. That first weekend we went shopping and, on the way, Mel looked upset. I asked her what was wrong, and she angrily said, "Now that whore Carrie is going to go after Todd." Carrie was Mel's close friend, but Mel always referred to her as a slut and home-wrecker. I asked Mel why, and she sternly said, "Why do you think?" I assumed it was because Mel always referred to Carrie as a promiscuous snake and let it go.

Everything seemed great, but Mel had bad news; she told me her mom was in hospice. She told me her mom was glad to hear Mel and I were back together. She liked me, as did the rest of her family. When we visited, I told her not to worry about Mel and that I would take care of her. She said she knew I would and thanked me. Not long after, she passed away. I did what I could to comfort Mel and her dad. We got Gary to come out and start hunting again. Something he hasn't done in maybe forty years. The family pooled some money together and got him some gear. We figured hunting might help him focus on something positive and keep his mind off things. I guess it worked because six months later, he started dating and met someone. He also sold the family home and bought a condo and a new Cadillac. Mel and her sister were unhappy about him seemingly moving on too quickly and spending their inheritance. I heard all the bickering, but I didn't join in on any of it. I was glad he was happy.

Not long after Mel came back, I asked Gary for permission. I did this at my work, where he also worked part-time. Gary and Tim (one of the company's owners) had been friends for years. Tim also attended Mel's first wedding many years ago, so it's like a family business. Gary gave me his blessing, but afterward, he also told me something very important. But because of the nature of the subject, I tried to forget it. It was an awkward part of the conversation that I forgot until early May 2021, later in the story.

That weekend we took a trip upstate and stayed at a nice hotel on the bay. I arranged to stay in the same hotel and room we had on our first trip together five years earlier when Mel was 33, and I was 38. The room number was 338. I think it was just a coincidence the first time, and we believed it was a sign for us. When we arrived, the room had a trail of rose petals leading to the bed, two small bottles of wine, chocolates, and a lovely handwritten card. It was a beautiful room with a great view of the bay. I told Mel I wanted to see the sunset before dinner, so we went for a drive. We got to the spot, then hiked down a trail to a scenic lookout where we watched the sunset, and I proposed. She said yes. It was a great weekend.

Because of our struggles in the past, I knew Mel had a lower libido than I did. We still struggled, but I was accepting and did not push. We talked about it and thought maybe it was the birth control pills. Mel didn't want kids; I already had three and didn't want anymore, so we agreed on a vasectomy. It would get her off the pills and may help our sex life. If it didn't help, I thought at least I could leave it in when those occasions did happen. So, I made the appointment. Mel stood by me the whole time and even snipped the cord. I was sore for a while, but after the healing period, we got to work. I didn't care for it, but considering the convenience factor, it was worth it. It was an improvement for us but nothing dramatic.

Mel always hated the old house, and I did too. She told me that she didn't want to live in that house, so it was either a complete remodel and addition or a new home. I was game. We spent the next two years in the process. At first, we planned a remodel and addition, but quotes were as high as a new home, and there would be more risk of going over budget. So, a new home it was. Having a construction background and being an engineer, I designed the house myself. I ran the numbers and ensured I could afford it myself, but lenders were tough and required both of our names to be on the mortgage. Also, everyone knows you cannot buy anything significant and must watch your spending during the process. Which in itself can be stressful and challenging. We couldn't afford a driveway or a deck, but I figured we could add those later.

The new home was built on the property while we lived in the old house near the front. There was a transition period where we needed a place to stay a couple of weeks, so they could demo the old home and put the final touches on the new home. We ended up staying with her dad and stepmom in their condo. Demo day came, and we watched the old house get torn down. Twenty minutes later, the old house was transformed into a trash pile and hauled out in large dump trucks. About a week later, we got the keys and were excited. Even though we had a new bedroom set scheduled to be delivered the next day, we couldn't wait and slept on the new carpet that night. The next day, after the bedroom set came, we went shopping for a few appliances, mirrors, and some décor. We also had to pick out window treatments. I installed a new water softener, filter system, and garage door openers over the next few weeks. Typical new house stuff, easy but time-consuming. Life was good, but it was hectic as well.

As spring comes, Mel suggested we get some chickens. I agreed, but first, we needed to revamp the old chicken coop. It was a fun project we did together. We ended up getting six hens and two ducks. We were always busy on the farm, and working together was enjoyable. We were also busy working in the garden. I built a dozen raised beds from the deck material I salvaged from the old house. We ran a water line out there, fenced it off, and made other finishing touches. It was a lot of work but come harvest time; it was worth it. Right before we had the house built, we worked together renovating a loft in one of the barns for her cats. That was a fun project as well.

A few months went by, and one day our neighbor George told us he was getting a new fence put up and wanted to tie it into our old corral fence. The old corral fence was on our property, so I told him no. When I initially moved in, another neighbor told me George was a bully, but I never had problems with him. Probably because I always said yes. I guess hearing "no" was his trigger, so this started arguments and me having the property line surveyed. I guess the survey did not matter to him as he kept yelling at me when I was outside. He even ordered a custom sign with my name on it and posted it where we and any guests we had over would see it. The texts he sent Mel and me were crazy, and we saved them all. I eventually called the police, and George took the sign down with my name on it. Then he painted "xxxxxx sucks" on the roof of one of his outbuildings. People that came over would see and ask about it. It sucked. So we planned to plant a bunch of trees and bushes to keep the sightline down. A six-foot privacy fence would not do much because our house sets high. We needed at least twelve feet. When planting time came, George saw us and came out. He walked across his property, leaned against his fence post, and continually harassed us while we planted trees for a couple of hours. Clearly, he was not mentally stable. For the most part, we ignored him as best we could, but it certainly didn't help our stress levels. He even put an offensive political flag on the corner of his property, but because our driveway and mailbox were close, it looked like my flag. He even put a camera on it so I could not touch it without him calling the cops, which I'm sure is exactly what he wanted. Every time we got the mail, it would take pictures or videos of us. Not cool, but the police said if the camera is on his property and not pointing inside our house, there isn't anything they can do. So I moved our mailbox to the other side of the driveway. Life was hectic and stressful. Things were about to break.

THREE

SOMETHING DIFFERENT (AUGUST 2019 - NOVEMBER 2019)

IT WAS near the end of August, and after some fine words with the neighbor, I remember walking around outside the house with Mel, and she said, "I think I want something different." When questioned about it, she blew it off and didn't elaborate. I never thought much about it, but it stuck with me. The next thing I know, I am lying in bed and noticed what appeared to be her masturbating under the blankets next to me. At first, I was a little confused, but then I was quickly turned on, and I discreetly took care of myself as I watched. I watched her the next couple of nights and thought, how could I approach her about this? I want to be part of this somehow. This could be the start of something new and exciting for us. Something I waited a long time for.

I was excited and daydreamed of the possibilities. I stopped by the flower shop on the way home from work. When I entered the house, Mel saw the flowers and asked, what are those for? I said we are celebrating! Concerned, she asked me what we were celebrating. I said you found your libido! I was excited and happy, but she had a worried look. I told her I noticed what she was doing in bed and asked if I could join. She said okay and nothing else. I assumed she was likely embarrassed and didn't want to ruin anything before it started, so I kept my mouth shut.

Showered and shaved, which is how Mel liked me, I rushed to bed early that night, not knowing what to expect. Normally I slept in my underwear, but not this time. I got into bed, slid over to her side, and spooned her. As I did, Mel lifted her leg and pulled me in tight. She kept her pajamas on and would work on herself under those. I thought she felt shame and needed to take small steps out of her comfort zone. I told her everything was ok and nothing wrong with going slow. I didn't push her, it was still exciting, and I wanted to see where this would lead, so we continued. Mel used several layers of bedding; a sheet, a custom weighted blanket I bought for her, a comforter on top of that, and sometimes even another blanket. So once I got in there and spooned, my hands could not get anywhere fast. I kept them on my side and would massage her as she did her thing on her side. Mel started by gripping me with one hand while the other played with herself and would alternate play by pushing me down for more access to herself. I could feel the in and out motion of fingers. She would hold, squeeze, and lightly touch me, teasing me, gripping harder as she built herself up. I could hear and feel her breathing increase, then finally shake when her moments hit, maybe fifteen to twenty minutes apart. Some were light, and some were heavy. This went on with me for two to three hours every night. Whenever I tried to slide my hand near Mel's working space, she would stop playing, pull away and say, "What are you doing?" and that she was sleeping or trying to sleep. She denied doing anything and claimed to be sleeping. I was shocked because it was very evident what we were doing. I didn't understand the denial and secrecy. I could only assume this was a game, or she was ashamed and still needed time. I would let it go because it wasn't the time or place for an argument. A few moments later, I could feel her hand slowly sliding back to working position. I told myself that if I played her game, she would gradually open up, and things would improve over time. Things were still crazy hot in bed. After doing this, I anticipated intercourse, but Mel said she didn't need that every time and would give me blowjobs or handjobs to get me off. At first, I tried every time because I thought she should be ready, but I was continually rejected. I thought that was weird because I didn't understand how your partner could get built up like that and not want intercourse. I wondered why she wasn't respecting me in bed but kept telling myself everyone was different and tried to be accommodating, but it wasn't easy. Mel didn't like to talk about it. She was demanding without making demands. I struggled to understand this side of her. She claimed it hurt and every other excuse you could imagine. Maybe fifty percent of the time would result in a BJ or HJ. I believe only once or twice a session turned into sex, which was good, so I'm not sure what the problem was. Our sessions happened nearly every night for about eight months, only skipping on the heaviest flow day during what she called shark week. She would only work her top half on the lighter days, and I was in because she still wore the pajamas. The only missed times were nights we argued about it, which we started to do, but she would still do it. That bothered me, especially if I didn't fall asleep right away. This created a few good arguments, but the first one was the one that did it for me. I kept thinking it was a game, but I was growing tired of the secrecy, so I pushed for answers one night. Mel looked at me with disdain and swore she wasn't doing anything. I was shocked at how serious she was. It was like I was talking to another person. She would have let it end us right then and there. Maybe that's how I should have handled it. Being told blatant lies by the person I loved was so confusing. I was speechless, but ultimately, I didn't think it was worth ruining what we had over her lying about toys and masturbation, so I caved and let it go. At this point, it wasn't about the toys or self-pleasure anymore; it was about the lying and gaslighting. I began to occasionally sleep on the couch or in the guest bedroom to avoid the gaslighting.

Another thing that bothered me was Mel would continue herself after using me, telling me she was done. Hours and hours a night. I couldn't believe it. I couldn't stay awake that long watching. Did she even sleep? Anytime I came to bed, all I had to do was whisper goodnight, and she would say goodnight no matter the time. She took sleeping pills but never really slept. It was bizarre, but I knew nothing of sleeping pills or any pills for that matter. Mel would get into bed between 8-9 p.m. and get up for work around 7 a.m. On the weekends, she would typically still get into bed early but sleep till 10-11 a.m. That's a lot of time in bed, but I still loved our sessions. I kept asking her to share more, open up more, and take the next step. She wouldn't talk about it, but I hoped she would hear me and act on it later.

Then Mel started using her hands. She has unusually small hands and a slender fist. I had joked with her before that a lesbian would love her. I am sure the women she was with most certainly did. Anyway, while spooning her and between her legs, she would take me, push me down to make room, and then go in herself. I could feel the point at which the widest part of her fist popped in the way her body would reflex. The images in my head of what she was doing just kept turning me on. When she finished inside, I could feel her again when the widest part came out.

When I tried for sex after, Mel said she was too sore. So I started to take care of myself, and she reached over and put her arm on my chest. When I touched her hand, I could feel her stickiness. I wondered how far she was going, so I lightly touched her hand, wrist, and up her arm, feeling for when the stickiness stopped. It was maybe three inches after the wrist, probably as far as she could.

She knew what I was doing and didn't say anything. This happened often. Sometimes when she was finished with me, I would watch her for a while with her back to me, and she would get both hands involved from both sides. I thought it was hot and mysterious at the time, never knowing what she would do. It had me racing to bed every night. Things were still crazy hot in bed. But it was also weird because Mel wasn't taking any steps to open up more, and I didn't know how to make things better. I told her we needed something smaller than her hand and long enough to reach where she wanted and wouldn't get sore. Mel claimed not to know what I was talking about and said the stickiness on her hand was sweat from holding it between her legs. I knew that was a lie, but I didn't want to argue anymore. She did say she was willing to look at some toys, so I thought that should be a good step forward.

The next evening while sitting on the couch, we talked briefly. I told Mel I felt we were on top of the world. We have a new house, good jobs, everything was going great, and the nightly exploration had me on cloud nine. Although she was playing this game with me, I thought it was headed in a positive direction. Then we broke out the laptop and looked at some toys. My idea was to get something that would allow her to reach wherever she needed without using her hand and getting sore. Much to my surprise, she shot down everything and said nothing that went inside. As I sat in disbelief, Mel again claimed to be doing nothing but sleeping, so we ended up not getting anything. She had a vibrator we bought together a while ago, but it's a clit vibe. I suggested adding that to keep moving forward.

Frustrated with Mel's continuous gaslighting about her nightly routine, I downloaded an audio app on my phone that I set up to record at night. It was noise activated and had no time stamps. I started the audio recordings after my part of the sessions ended, usually around midnight to 1 a.m. I wasn't surprised to hear Mel move around, open the nightstand drawers, get out of bed multiple times a night for the bathroom, let the dog out, get a drink, etc. But nothing stuck out so far. Because Mel kept me up every night for hours, I started going to work later than my usual lateness. I always put in my time, which meant the later I came in, the later I would stay. That worked well for traffic, but my boss was noticing, and I felt I needed to explain a little of why. My boss is a cool guy, and I consider him a friend, so I wanted to pick his brain a little. I apologized for coming in late and told him Mel was keeping me up for hours a night, every night, and wondered if his wife went through anything like that. My boss and his wife are a few years older than us, so maybe his wife went through something. He said she did and remembered her inability to get enough of him during some phase of her life. I told him it wasn't like that with Mel. I said it was weird but hopefully headed in the right direction. I wasn't comfortable saying anything else, and he understood, so that was all I needed.

Mel called what we were doing Pretzeling. So, I began using the acronym PIVY which was... Penis in Vagina Yay. We Pretzeled all the time, but PIVY was hard to come by. One Wednesday evening after a pretzel session, I tried for sex but Mel rejected me and told me Friday. She offered a blowjob instead, and I looked forward to Friday. It didn't take long for me to learn that if I tried for sex, she would offer a blowjob, and if I asked for a blowjob, she would offer a handjob. When Friday evening came around, Mel again rejected me, promising for tomorrow evening, but ok to pretzel, of course. We did, and afterward, I took care of myself. Then I went out to the garage for a nightcap, and when I came back in, I turned on the voice recorder app and went to sleep. I didn't get to listen to the recording on Saturday, but just in case I got rejected again, I planned to set the recorder that evening. Saturday evening comes, and we both shower and get into bed. Mel wanted to get busy, but I suggested we pretzel then PIVY. I thought pretzeling was excellent foreplay. We did that night, and it was a night to remember. It was the first time she had shown me something she could do. After some pretzel play, Mel invited me on top. She was hotter and wetter than usual, which was nice. We were going at it for a little while, and then she curved her hips straight up. I pushed myself upwards with my toes staying all the way in, pushing down and applying pressure. I was hitting her cervix, so I assumed she liked that. I remembered her doing this in the past, but that wasn't everything. This time, Mel gave me a look like here goes nothing, and she picked her head up a little and twisted her abdomen, almost like she was trying to get up. The next thing I knew, I felt a powerful, tight stream of fluid hitting the side of me while in her that lasted for about five seconds. Normally Mel never got very wet, but this was over the top. I thought it must be leaving a huge puddle on the bed and checked with my hand and felt nothing. It was all on the inside. Only after I started thrusting did anything come out. It was extremely wet. The wet sloshing sound during thrusting was hot, and I had difficulty controlling myself. After thrusting most out, I didn't think she could immediately do it again. So, maybe something had to be built up. I had no idea. Afterward, I was like, wow, where did you learn? Wait, I don't want to know, but that was amazing, and I love you! When Mel got up and headed to the bathroom, I checked out the wet spot, and it was larger than a basketball, oval-shaped with spurts reaching out from the thrusting motions. I carefully leaned in to smell it, and I couldn't smell anything. I thought it was certainly not urine like porn shows. How could it be? It came from the inside. Mel was certainly not going to tell me anything, so I researched a little online but didn't find anything. I quickly gave up and just enjoyed it. From that point on, whenever we had sex, we grabbed a towel, and Mel was able to do it on demand. We would have fun for a while, saving the super wetness for last.

I thought Mel's nightly self-exploration, which is probably equal to half of her adult life, put her knowledge level higher than most. Mel never had children, so maybe that had something to do with it. Who knows? I don't know where it came from, and it didn't matter. It had nothing to do with an orgasm. Putting pressure on or squeezing something inside is what made it happen. I didn't ask questions because I wasn't sure I wanted to hear the answers. Besides, Mel wouldn't answer any of them. She was very conservative with me and didn't discuss what she liked or wanted in the bedroom. She was silent but demanding, and I followed her like a clueless and obedient dog waiting for my reward. Of course, I was part of the equation as well, but I don't think I'm anything special with my seven-inch pretzel stick, as Mel would call it. I cannot compete with an arm, though, so there were times I felt insecure. Watching porn usually made me feel better. I think I look good, especially on my 165-pound frame.

I went to the pole barn and listened to the audio recordings on Sunday. On the Saturday night recording, I listened to the sounds of us and the super-wet thrusting. I have never recorded us before, and it felt wrong to me. I never recorded us again. It was still hot, though. But it was the Friday night recording that was odd. Sometime after I went to sleep, she moved around in bed, made an umph sound, then a grit-your-teeth, hold-your-breath, whisper, "oh my god." Then a few seconds later was the same super wet thrusting noise she made with me on Saturday. It only went on for maybe ten or fifteen seconds. I listened to it many times and didn't hear anyone else in the room. I assumed it was a toy, and she wanted to see if she could still do the thing before attempting to do it with me. I looked around again for any of the toys she was using and still didn't find anything, but I think I found where she kept something. In her suitcase upstairs, I found a rolled-up towel, but when I unraveled it, there was nothing but the indentation of a large round cylinder shape that was once there. It seemed like Mel was always a step ahead of me. My problem was I usually went directly to her, asking questions about things, which gave her the heads up she needed to stay ahead of me. She continued to control the situation and kept her dark secret.

*(I believe I figured out Mel's super-wetness ability discussed in Chapter 10, Aftermath.)

For a while, it seemed to be working. We would have mild-blowing sex during the night and cuddle in the mornings. Both of us were aware that work was taking a toll on our physical and mental health, so we began to plan a vacation. Along with the wedding: we had finally completely settled on August 22nd to be our wedding date.

As for the vacation, we discussed getting a cabin. Both of us desperately wanted to go to Hawaii or Jamaica, but a 10k trip was definitely out of our budget. We were itching to get out of our everyday routines.

Every so often, I would try to suggest new things, but I was usually given no response. I tried to not let it discourage me, but a man could only do so much about it before he slowly started giving up. Mel noticed it too and has apologized for slacking even in the cuddling department. She was struggling again, but I tried my best not to let it get to me.

I have discovered that Mel had a particular fondness for a spot. Every time I would hit the spot, she would get so incredibly wet. It would drive me insane, and I made it my mission to make her that wet every time. We had gotten to the point where it was easier to openly talk about it—at least on my end. I just wanted to make her feel good. She was the master, and I was just a submissive toy in the bedroom. I decided to get her another toy, too. Something that would help her reach her spot without needing the recovery time. More than anything, I wanted to just... Watch her, but the recovery time was putting me out of the business. Mel agreed to look into it, and it warmed my heart to know she was receptive to my suggestions. I began feeling more and more in tune with her every day again… Or so I thought. I loved the thought of her using a vibrator while we cuddled, too.

Mel would often wait to "bounce back" for me after we'd have sex. I urged her not to. If she was sore, sure, but otherwise… I sort of enjoyed the thought of it and wanted to try it out before she wore herself out. Again, I tried to let her know that it would happen whenever she felt ready and wanted to try it out.

She made it her mission to tease me up, and it made me hard like nothing else ever had. I loved using her wetness for lube. I loved being held tight while she played, then she would tease and loosen a little. I could feel myself releasing almost instantly. She had many tricks up her sleeve; I loved the tapping and rubbing of the tip while she held tight. She had her way when it came to working around my tip and balls, as well as I loved it when she put her arm on my chest and I could feel the stickiness on her fingers, hand, and wrist. Mel, on the other hand, liked it when I held her in the morning. It was usually a concern of mine—that she would reject me. There had been a lot of rejection in the past, but thankfully not much as of late. I was getting to know what she liked and would try to be gentle and slow. I loved it when she told me what she liked.

Of course, that wasn't to say that there weren't still struggles. Every so often, she would shut down and wouldn't communicate. It seemed to be one of her main struggles—one that was all present, even when life seemed to be good. In moments like those, I tried letting her know that I felt unequal, inferior, self-conscious, and disappointed. She would always say she understood, but she didn't really. How could she have understood and still continued doing it?

I wished I knew what was going on in her head. I wanted to know everything; there wasn't anything she could tell me that would hurt me more than keeping it from me. I didn't care what it looked like, where, when, or whom it came from. I could easily see the guilt in her eyes most of the time, and I didn't like to see her that way.

Soon, there was the first Thanksgiving that we didn't spend together. I missed Mel more than words could describe, but I also felt like some distance between us could do us some good. Make us closer. Mel pondered spending Thanksgiving with her family while I traveled up north for the weekend. A hunting trip was exactly what I needed.

FOUR

SOMETHING WRONG (NOVEMBER 2019 – JANUARY 2020)

It was early November 2019 at the time, and my vacation was coming up soon. Every year I take a week off for deer hunting, and I have been hunting on the property since I have been on the farm. Mel had asked me to finally bring some of her stuff in from the pole barn, which I did on my time off. It was right after I brought her things in that the vibrations started. That night she touched me with it, and it was a new feeling for me. I don't know what it looked like because I have never seen it. She hid everything from me. I thought it might have been the vibrator I bought for her years ago, but it wasn't. She had used that one in the past on me, and it was louder and more aggressive, you could say. I could tell she did not like it because she would try to hold it tightly to muffle its operation. These toys were different.

As I got into bed that night and moved into position, I could feel her vibrating against me. I soon learned she would put the vibrator in her and leave it as she worked her top half. She would push me downward to gain room to pull it out between rounds and began lightly touching me with it, moving up and down and sometimes applying more pressure, especially when she was having an orgasm. Sometimes she would lightly touch my balls or under them with it. The whole time she did these things, I lightly massaged her and softly kissed her back while running my fingers through her hair. As she reached her orgasms, I sometimes pulled her hair or squeezed her ass tighter. Even though Mel never talked about it, I did what I thought she liked. Her pleasure was my pleasure. But whenever I moved my hand towards her working area, she would stop and ask what am I doing? Claiming she is trying to sleep. Of course, I was confused, but I continued to play her game because I wanted her to open up to me and not force anything. A few days later, I noticed something else she was using. This toy seemed more traditional for internal use but on the small side. How do I know? I could feel her start with the toy and then push her hand in with the toy. I could always feel her body reflex as the widest part of her fist went in and played, then out when finished. When she was in and playing, I could feel the toy poking my stomach through her lower back as I spooned her. It was a weird feeling, but the mental images kept turning me on. The visuals in my mind were strong. It was extremely compelling. I became obsessed, and Mel had me racing to bed every night, wondering what might happen next. I would daydream and get excited often throughout the day. I couldn't wait for what the next evening would hold.

We were good as long as I did not question anything that happened at night. All other aspects of life were good, but she always planned sex. Mel would reject me and tell me another day. On the nights we would have sex, she never wanted to pretzel first. I thought it was great foreplay, and the sex was intense after pretzeling. I assumed she wanted to protect her claims of not doing anything but sleeping. A little frustrating, but I'm not going to turn down sex. Mel would always set up candles, wine, and soft background music. The sex was always good but mostly vanilla. Not that there's anything wrong with that, but she shot down any suggestions I made to change things up. She never liked me going down on her as well, but when I did, she liked it. She said it wasn't me and claimed to be self-conscious about it. I tried to tell her she had nothing to worry about, but it didn't matter. I didn't understand, but it wasn't a big deal either. She also told me she didn't like any liquid touching her face. I thought that was strange, but it didn't bother me because she routinely swallowed anyway.

My gut kept telling me something was wrong, and it felt like I was living in the twilight zone. I wanted answers, so I decided to do some more snooping. I started with the audio recording app. The app would record anywhere from one to two hours during the night. I listened to the recordings on my drive to/from work, during lunch or breaks. I usually didn't hear much. She was extremely quiet and never moaned or anything. Pretty much just her breathing and vibrating noises in bed, along with nightstand drawers opening/closing and suspected devices being charged. Rosy would come in once or twice a night and let Mel know she had to go outside. Sometimes she would make her wait a few minutes for some reason. On one recording, I heard the sound of her opening a box, then plastic wrapping and plugging something into an outlet. Of course, my thought was she got a new toy. I wondered where she kept them and would quickly look around after she left for work. Eventually, I ran out of places to look and never found anything. She was very sneaky. In the mornings, she would wake up before me, so she probably did something with them. I concluded that she must take them to work with her. In the evenings, Mel would already be in bed when I went into the shower, but I would hear her running upstairs or downstairs while I was in the shower. I suspected getting a device that was charging somewhere. When I came out of the shower, she would lie in bed as if she had never left. I knew she was hiding stuff and lying to me, but at the time, I felt it was just toys and not worth all the fighting.

One day while looking around, I noticed she had a vibrating razor in the bathroom closet. It was in a cup with other razors and girl stuff. The vibrating razor handle was clean compared to the dust-covered others in the cup, and it had a razor on it that looked many years old with packed-on make-up. Clearly, it wasn't the razor she normally uses. Plus, there were already two regular razors in the shower and two on the bathtub sill. I turned it on and immediately determined it was not the same ones she uses in bed. It had a different tone and feel. I checked to see what kind of battery it took and put it away. A couple of days later, Mel took another bath. She was on her period and, for some reason, liked to take baths during that time. The next day I thought about checking the vibrating razor again. The handle was shiny clean with the same old make-up-packed razor on it. I decided to check the battery. I had to squeeze the handle to screw the cap off, and when I looked, it had a new battery. I thought it wasn't a big deal, but it confirmed the lying. I went to put it back and noticed blood on my hand. I thought maybe I touched the blade and cut myself, but I looked at the make-up-packed razor, and nothing was there. I was confused. Where did it come from? I rinsed my hand off and squeezed the handle again. There was blood coming out of the molded crevices in the handle. I had no doubts about what she was using it for then. I desperately wanted to catch her lying so she would have no choice but to come clean. When I asked Mel about it, she claimed to use it to shave down there and dripped blood on the handle. The excuses were terrible. I tried explaining to her that what she was doing was ok and she didn't need to lie to me, but she never admitted anything. She claimed I was obsessed with sex and wanted her to have sex with me all the time. Sure, I would like to have sex a lot with my partner. But that wasn't true because there was a year in our past that we only had sex maybe three times. Looking back, I'm not sure why. Partly because I assumed she had a low libido, and I didn't want to push her and wind up like we did the first time. But also, because we were just busy having fun spending time together, working on the farm, both had full-time jobs and building a new house. Just lots of things going on. Other than that busy year, normal "struggles" were maybe once a month. It went up to two or three times a month during this strange time. Which I think is extremely low considering what we were doing every night. Whenever I approached her about something, she excused it and altered her habits. Exactly what people do who are hiding something from you. You cannot ask them about it; they will gaslight you. They are the ones hiding it from you. I didn't think anything else was going on, but things continued to escalate.

On Thanksgiving Day, Mel and I hosted my family for the first time in our new home. After the typical pretzel session and rejection the night before, we argued in the early morning, so I went upstairs to sleep. I didn't fall asleep until late morning and ended up sleeping until an hour before my family was to show up. I didn't help much. It was a bad time, but we got through it. Afterward, I went upstate for the annual rifle deer hunt with my friends that long weekend. I was worried about her and us the whole time but tried to have fun. I came home a day early without any deer but good stories. Mel wanted to re-connect when I returned and planned an evening with candles, baby oil, and massages. Sounds nice. We got naked, and we both got nice massages. So far, so good until I tried to initiate sex and was rejected. I was really confused, and we sat next to each other holding hands, both still naked, and she said it doesn't always have to be about sex. It was an abnormal rejection situation. Afterward, Mel told me she wanted to switch sides of the bed, with her closer to the door. I didn't understand her wanting to switch sides, but I told her no; the man needed to be closer to the door in case someone broke in. Needless to say, Mel's "re-connecting" evening didn't go well.

Now into December, things were getting worse. I tried hard to keep us together. The nightly pretzeling continued, and our arguments increased. I was never jealous or controlling and never looked at her phone, but she started to tell me to check her phone. I briefly looked at it while sitting beside her, but it felt awkward. Mel had an iPhone, and I didn't know anything about them. She took it back after a minute or two anyway. Besides, anything Mel wanted to hide would be hidden or deleted, so it wasn't worth it. One evening while sitting on the couch, we argued about the nightly sessions, and again she still claimed she was doing nothing but sleeping, and I was delusional. Mel said I was psychotic from smoking weed. She looked it up on her phone and showed me the symptoms, which included delusions and paranoia. I knew what she was doing and was fed up with her gaslighting, so I thought I should make her listen to my audio file of her masturbating. But how would I cover for secretly recording her? Then I remembered Mel told me I could record her sleeping in one of our arguments. So, I thought that could be my out if she gets upset about it. So, I told her I had an audio recording of her doing shit after I went to sleep. She looked worried and demanded to listen, so I plugged in the earphones and let her listen. The look on her face said holy shit, he caught me, but afterward, she claimed to hear nothing. She then got very angry that I was recording her. I reminded her that she had previously told me it was ok. She replied that I needed to tell her I was doing it first. I said that didn't make sense because if I told her I was recording, she wouldn't do anything. It ended with me regrettably deleting the recordings and telling her I wouldn't do it again. I thought her knowing I knew was enough and let it go. After all, it was just her lying about her self-pleasure, and I wanted to keep us together and grow, not pull us apart.

A couple of days later, Mel surprised me with hockey tickets she claimed to have received as a gift from her boss. We would be going with her sister Kelly and her brother-in-law, Steve. Mel knew I was not too fond of crowds or going downtown, but hockey can be fun to watch, so I went. It was a dark time, though, as we had argued the night before. Mel appeared to have no issues with what was going on in our lives. I wore a hoodie the whole time and didn't say much. It wasn't the best time. I was sitting next to my fiancé, who lies to me. But I got through it.

Kelly and Steve are weird, but everyone has their quirks. A few weeks earlier, they visited, and Kelly talked about bukkake and cuckolding. I knew what bukkake was from porn but not the other word. I had to look it up. I guess it is where the male partner watches other guys (bulls) have sex with their female partner. That is some fucked up shit (but little did I know what I was living, I guess those were hints). After they left, Mel told me that her sister could only have an orgasm during sex if she had a vibrator in her ass. I'm not sure where that came from, but I didn't need to know. Mel very rarely had orgasms during sex, so maybe it was hereditary. I never questioned it because I heard it was common. My ex had one every time, but what could I do besides whatever Mel wanted? I was good with anything she desired of me, which was never much. I tried, but Mel was never responsive to my suggestions. One time I asked Mel about anal, and she said no-no-no and that she has "fissures" or tiny tears in her ass caused by constipation from the side effect of pain pills. I'm not sure I bought that one, but she did clog the toilet almost every time. Mel even bought a personal plunger because she didn't like the others we had. She would carry it to whatever bathroom she was using. I thought it was funny.

A couple weeks later, Mel surprised me during a nightly pretzel session and wanted sex. A rare and pleasant surprise. We were both ready after an hour or so of pretzeling, and she wanted it hard and fast. While directing me to hurry on top, I thought I might turn the tables and reject her at that moment. Yeah, right. Who am I kidding? In it goes. At first, I remember feeling a vibration somewhere inside but not directly. I wasn't about to stop and talk about it. I hit hard as she directed, and Mel's body started to shake after just a few minutes, which was my cue. Afterward, as we caught our breaths, I said to Mel, look how great that was. It didn't take long, and we must do that more often after pretzeling. Mel agreed but would never act. While still on top and inside, I could again feel the vibrations. I told Mel I felt something and tried to move around a little to get a better feel, but she pushed me off and said she had to use the bathroom and that I was crazy. I'm not sure why, but that was the only time that happened.

During the first couple weeks of December, Mel had mentioned a few times she had to talk to me about something. She kept putting it off and acting like it was not a big deal, so I took it as much. Then she said we needed to talk one evening, and I figured this was the time. We sat on our kitchen stools facing each other, knees touching and holding hands. She started crying. I told her everything would be okay, and she could tell me anything. She said I need to tell you something. She said she was…long pause…(changed mind at the last minute) addicted to pain pills. I was confused because I knew that. I said that wasn't what you were going to tell me. I was getting black-market pills for her for a long time because I felt bad about her doctor cutting her back. She then said it was worse than I thought, and she would take ten a day and be out in three days, but I knew she was just scrambling to cover. That wasn't what she planned on telling me, and because she decided against telling me, there was no getting it out of her. I didn't know what to do. I loved her and planned to spend the rest of my life with her, but something was wrong.

The day of my work Christmas party arrives. After Mel left for work, I woke up and went to the bathroom. Mel usually left her clothes on the bathroom floor, but this time she purposely laid them out for me to see. Her underwear stared at me as I sat on the toilet. She rubbed a hole straight through, and the material around it was so thin that you could see through it. I was happy that she would display them for me. I thought it was a sign of affection and her taking steps to open up to me while teasing me simultaneously. I took a pic and sent her a text. I thanked her and told her they are now referred to as my favorite underwear and not to throw them out. I was happy and excited, but Mel responded by denying everything and saying they were just old. She even later dared to tell me the hole was not in the right spot. I knew she was lying, but I wasn't going to argue. I was disappointed and confused more than anything else.

After work, I met Mel in the parking lot at the banquet hall my work rented for the Christmas party. It was a nice place with a cabin feel, exposed beams, and a large stone fireplace. About a dozen tables were in the large room, each seated eight people. We picked a table, ordered some drinks, and relaxed and chatted with other guests. Another coworker enters with his girl and sits at our table across from Mel and me. Everyone called him Grump because of his negative attitude and seemingly permanent frown. Ann was his long-time girlfriend; she was cute and seemed cool. As we small-talked, I wondered why she was with Grump. They were together for about as long as Mel and me. They were around our age, but we never hung out or talked much because Grump was a drunkard and a dick. Not long into dinner, Richard, an older coworker at our table, noticed that Grump was staring at Mel with his sad frown face. Richard doesn't have a filter, so he yelled across the table and asked Grump why he was frowning and looking at Mel. Just as I noticed, Grump broke his trance and replied that he was staring out the window behind us. I took note but let it go. I may have been busy checking out Ann, so I had no room to say anything. After dinner, I noticed what looked like Grump trying to play footsie with Mel, but he said he was stretching his legs. Everyone was drinking, talking, and having a good time, so I didn't think too much about it. Leaving seemed awkward and uncomfortable with the hugs and handshakes but being an introvert, that always felt awkward for me. I had no reason to think anything was happening at the time, so I chalked it up to my insecurities. Mel and I were excited to get back home and into bed, so that's where my mind went.

I kept trying things to get Mel to open up and tell me. I decided since we were supposed to get married in the fall, I would get the wedding band part of the ring. She already had an engagement ring but thought it would be fitting to have both, and besides, it may guilt her into telling me so we can move past whatever it is and move forward. We went to the jewelers, and she picked out what she wanted. We later learned that to get the ring sized; she would lose some diamonds because of her tiny fingers. I guess it didn't bother her to wear it the way it was, so she decided to leave it. It was beautiful, and she was happy, but as it turned out, it was not enough to get her to tell me anything.

Christmas came and went. We hosted her family, which was a little stressful, but we got through it, and our nightly sessions continued.

AUGUST 2019 – NOVEMBER 2019

The two of us recalled a time three years ago when we were heading to Gatlinburg. Mel liked her hair back then, and she suddenly found herself wanting to get back to that era. She planned to make an appointment with Natalie, but money was always an issue. I thought she looked good either way.

At last, she ended up asking Natalie if she could do her hair that weekend; just highlights and her bangs cut. No special treatments or extra colour or cuts to keep the costs low. She also wanted to go to Gatlinburg. Mel told Kelly too bad we couldn't go to Key West with them around Christmas time. That was a great time to go, and I couldn't agree more. We also debated on trying some pour painting. Mel claimed that mine would turn out better than hers because I was a creative genius, but I begged to differ.

The next night, I woke up at almost 5 and had trouble getting back to sleep. Mel slept well, but she said she wished we could have snuggled. After last night, however, I had no strength left to even snuggle. But we were going to tonight. We both agreed that last night was intense, and we definitely needed a break in the form of some cuddling tonight. I didn't know how it was possible, but sex simply continued getting better and better, and I found myself unable to get enough. As good as it was, however, there were still times of disagreement and bickering that would have our distance from each other, but it wouldn't last for longer than a few hours. One of us would usually apologize, and we would quickly make up. I'd apologize about things, but Mel would usually assure me there was nothing to be sorry about. She just thought she had done something wrong, but that couldn't have been further from the truth. The truth was, I was just tired most of the time, and it would sometimes get to me. Most of the time, Mel and I were both more than excited about the long, much-needed weekends.

Mel would often complain about difficulties that she encountered with people in her life and I tried my best to be there for her—like the supportive man I was trying to be. At one point, most of her mind was wrapped around Carrie. She couldn't tell what she had done to her, but Carrie had totally ghosted her. I couldn't help but wonder why either. Mel made up her mind; she was done being there for Carrie whenever shit went down in her love life. Carrie was almost fifty; surely she could figure it out for herself. Mel's feelings were hurt, but I knew her well enough to know that her mind wasn't going to change. It was starting to sound like a regular occurrence to me, and Mel was definitely going to need her kratom.

Afterward, I took some time off to build a deer hunting blind. It was a fun project that helped me get my mind off things. Her father helped me–and I didn't mind the old man's company. Mel and I had broken the ground exactly one year ago. It was crazy how a single year could go by so fast yet so slowly at the same time.

The year itself was filled with pain on Mel's end. Some days would be worse than others–I would often recommend to her that she tried her best to take it slow so it wouldn't feel bad. Mel tried the best she could, but we both knew that it would be hard. She wasn't the kind of a person to just take things easy. It was both a blessing and a curse on her end.

Any driver in the area knew the morning struggles of getting to work. Myself and Mel included. Mel went through her usual motion of getting the kratom after work and getting home later than normal. That day, she made it to work only to have her meeting canceled, and she spent the morning in the bathroom, practically shitting her brains out. Her nerves got the best of her, as did her stomach.

I asked her once if she could have everything she ever wanted– besides more money at work or the ability to retire now, what else would her heart desire? Her answer was simple–one you would expect from a lot of women. A couple of goats (maybe a little less simple, I suppose), another puppy, a couple of kittens, flower bulbs, and of course, some good loving from her man. The latter was exactly what I hoped she would have said. I agreed–mine included a kennel and a pen of goats the next year. Along with a deck, marriage, and a good ol' vacation. Then it hit me.

"How will we vacation with all those animals?" I asked her. "Who will take care of them?"

"Better buy a farm hand," she joked in return.

The bulbs were an ongoing thing for her. She hoped to order them from Lowes or Home Depot. Considering all of our financial struggles and living on a budget, she wanted my permission to order them on CC. She took living on a budget to another level, often eating just cucumbers for lunch. One more week before she got her meds, she told me, and then she would finally be able to help with rocks or anything heavy that I may need help with. In order to be able to do that, I warned her that she'd have to start eating more than just cucumbers. Budget or not. Mel retorted with something that caught me off guard, telling me that I may want to start writing my vows to her. She said I had a year.

For the first time in a long time, I didn't have a clue how to respond to her.

The 18th of September 2019 was a rough one. Not only was it another long day at work—one that I didn't even bother preparing myself a lunch for, but it was also the weekend we were supposed to be getting married on. A vacation next week was supposed to follow, but neither of those ended up happening. At least tomorrow was a happy pill day. That had to count for something, didn't it?

Her stomach was continuously getting upset over the meetings that she continued to have; it was something that she would mention on a regular basis and something that occasionally worried me. Thankfully, at least she was getting her meds soon. I was excited to see the improvement the medication would bring her, especially on the day when she stated she was actually going to pick them up. I couldn't wait to get back home and see her.

Her name popped up on the screen of my phone with a simple message saying, *"ETA?"*

Nothing out of the ordinary. I responded with, *"15 minutes."*

"K. Better tell my boyfriend to leave now. Lol." Another message

popped up. A small smile curved my lips. It was another attempt of hers to be humorous–or so I thought at the time.

"Or back in the drawer," I responded jokingly. Looking back, I can't believe just how naive I was. Mel responded with nothing more but a smiley face. What else could she have said?

The next weekend was the last weekend to practice before hunting. Mel decided to ask her dad to come over and help with the practice, and I wholeheartedly agreed. In attempts to save up money, she also insisted that we put the meat in the freezer, even if we took a large doe early. "In the long run, it would save us money," she said. There was logic in her words, so I couldn't help but agree.

Something that started happening often was her asking me if I would come home early and at what time. Again, I didn't think anything of it–how sweet of her to want me to get home as soon as possible. Naively, I'd ask her what she wanted to do after work, and she'd often suggest date nights. I thought it was sweet; a sign that we were doing well and definitely on our way to being even more connected. I loved the feeling, and I never wanted it to stop. She told me we only had each other and that I was her rock and mate for life. It took us a while to get there, but we were finally stable and everything seemed to be flowing well.

Slow but real–and it was all that mattered. Or so I thought, at least.

The sex was incredible, too. Some mornings I wanted her to stay a little extra longer in bed with me for obvious reasons, but she would usually refuse to because of the traffic. It was one thing that we always complained about–one thing that we seemed to always be stuck in. She'd usually make a promise to suck me off in the evening if she had to leave me to take care of my hard-ons in the morning. Likewise, I also quite enjoyed taking care of her myself, especially when the stress of work got the best of her, which often resulted in terrible stomach aches that she couldn't get rid of.

At one point, the continuous work to earn as much money as possible began getting to me, too. Mel was banging hot and she was incredible when it came to fucking, but some days, it just wasn't happening on my end. I assured her that she did an amazing job when it came to handling me, and she seemed to accept that as a fact. If there was one thing about Mel… It was that she was always willing to try again.

In fact, she'd shower me with 'I love you's,' which often had me suspecting that she wanted something. She assured me that it was nothing like that–she was merely appreciating how solid our relationship was, and cherishing all the good that she had in her life. She did have a lot of good things. A dog, chickens, ducks, cats, and a farm… A newer car, a solid job, and a beautiful new home, along with a family that loved her.

Things only seemed to get worse at work for Mel. She would often be in tears at work, telling me she didn't know what she was doing. I tried to be supportive–urge her to ask questions, write things down, and try to learn, but she seemed to be discouraged easily. She didn't know what or how to ask–that was half her problem. Her boss wouldn't let her write stuff down and would flip through all kinds of stuff, often causing her to have breakdowns. Again, I presented a solution–to record conversations, but Mel claimed that she explored that option, too.

She tried to stay as positive as possible, but she'd often suggest escapes. Such as taking the dog and going up north on a Friday night to look at the colors… To stay somewhere cheap. Maybe go to a couple of different cider mills. With how crazy my work schedule was, that often wasn't doable, but I'd make it up to her in different ways, like getting *Goats for Dummies* for her, or sleeping naked, cuddling her, and having her use my wetness for lube. The thought of seeing how long I could hold out was exciting to me, while Mel had different kinds of fantasies. The ones that involved the goat pen and other animals.

"Bestiality?" I joked. "That's a bit much for me."

The joke didn't seem to sit right with Mel, so I apologized and promised her that we would have our very own goats soon. Regardless of my words, work seemed to be still having a negative impact on both our lives, especially during our night routines. I couldn't wait for it to be over, just so that we could get back to focusing on ourselves. Mel agreed that we were both shot these days, and we needed some well-deserved time for ourselves. Pronto.

While struggling with the stress of work, we also had issues with our neighbor that drained us additionally. Mel dreamed of planting hundreds of trees along the property line to secure our home. I liked the idea, too. Hunting wasn't an option right now either—at least not before tension with the neighbor calmed down a bit. Mel's dad came over often just to keep an eye on things while we were gone for work, and we'd leave his key on the scaffolding behind the horse bar, right in the middle. The tension seemed to subdue on a random weekend when I knocked the neighbour down, once and for all, and was deemed Mel's hero.

It was just the way life functioned—something I learned from a young age. You had to stand up to bullies and do the right thing. It always paid off. You just couldn't sit back and let them walk all over you. It wasn't a good feeling, so it was more than worth it. Every penny in the case.

Sadly, none of the trees that Mel imagined in her head were available for fall planting. We had to have our order placed before November 1st. At least 200, we believed, but as much as 400 for the spring planting. Our property would look amazing—both of us had the vision in our heads already. Having all sorts of animals around and growing old on that property. We were eager to make it a dream come true in every aspect. For now, until next summer, we would be seeing our crappy neighbor and his bratty kids, just as they would be seeing our property. Neither of us liked it, but for now, it was just the way it had to be. Nothing to be done about it.

Mel struggled with poor sleep. By the time she would fall asleep, her alarm would go off in an hour or two. She needed frequent refills just to be able to function normally. It didn't help that her work was busier, and it was getting increasingly more difficult to take time off. Ambien and Norco were what kept her life good, apparently. Mel also tried her best to keep working out, even when she had no motivation to do so. I saw her efforts, and it was hard to stop thinking about her, even when she struggled. That was my curse. I often wished I would be able to get back home and know exactly what she needed, but there were things I couldn't ever help with.

Nothing aside from medication that she continuously struggled with could help.

It began affecting our sex life even more so. I felt as if she was keeping her sexual drive to herself, leaving none for us, and it was something I tried hard to tap into. I wasn't trying to take "her" time away; instead, I just want to share a brief part of it, which would bring us closer and make us both feel good. She would often shut me down and turn me away, which felt like we were going backward, and it made me feel alone. I was proud of the good, but slow progress that she was making, and I didn't want to scare her into secrecy. I loved her more every day, and I wished to grow and learn everything about her and would have liked to keep it that way. It often seemed like she wanted to keep that stuff to herself, and I didn't think that was the way relationships should work. We needed to grow with each other; not just coexist and give each other pleasure purely based on whether they deserve it, feel a duty to the relationship, or feel bad.

I wanted her to desire me, just as I desired her.

Mel took my words into consideration, but there was no doubt that she was depressed. She struggled with her sleep and medication immensely, and there was nothing I could do to help. Her depression stemmed from herself alone, she claimed. I made an attempt to focus more on the mustang and hunting, which caused additional worry on her end.

She wanted to make me happy. She more than once stated that it was a constant thought on her mind, but she couldn't help the feeling that I wasn't feeling the same way she did. It was hard for Mel; she was left with a feeling that I would never be fully happy. What I perceived as rejections had nothing to do with me, she claimed but had everything to do with her struggle with sleep.

On a level, I understood that.

I felt a similar way. I wanted to make her happy in every way, but actions and reality told me I was lacking. I often tried to crack open that door and I got shut out. I hoped that someday we would get to the point where we would be able to be open with each other entirely, but it would take a lot of time and she would have to take the steps to be able to open up and talk to me about these things. There was absolutely nothing to be embarrassed or ashamed about with me. I loved her in every way possible, with all my being, and I wanted to leave the time and place of that talk to her. I believed that once we fully understood each other's wants and needs then we could finally live in bliss.

Mel was desperate for medication. She'd often ask Kelly to help her out–to have Steve bring her one more Ambien for the night and she would give it back to her on the weekend. She knew that Kelly just got her scripts filled on Tuesday, even if Kelly said she didn't have any. Mel decided she wouldn't be doing any more favours for Kelly then–like watching her dog which was something she did on a regular basis. If she couldn't help her out with just one Ambien, then Mel would return in the same measure. It didn't matter that

Kelly tried to explain that she was trying to cut back, but Mel was done. She was done helping them out.

She soon brought up getting married again. The HR told her their health insurance was going up 43% as they were switching providers, and she was desperately hoping that it wouldn't mess with her doctors.

"One more reason to get married," she said, uncertain about her current place any longer. 22nd of August 2020. She decided that would be our wedding date. She worked hard to convince herself that things will be okay. Every day was a struggle to stay positive–a struggle that she tried to hide from me... But it was getting more and more difficult for her to do so. No matter how much I tried to assure her that it couldn't be further from the truth, this was something that she refused to discuss with me because she didn't want to burden me with her depressive thoughts. Her actions had the very opposite effect; her keeping things bottled up inside of her instead of opening up to me and speaking about what was on her mind were all things that would eventually cause distance between us... The distance that I so desperately fought to keep away.

DECEMBER 2019

After my trip, we settled to start off fresh from here and move forward through any issues we had. That included me talking to a counselor, too. Local psychological services had good reviews, but I couldn't seem to find them on my approved provider list. It sucked that the best-rated places weren't on my approved list. I wanted to get past all of my issues and move forward. Mel was more than supportive, telling me that she would help in any way she could.

She started stepping out of her comfort, too. Cutting out Dr. Pepper and regular pops was the first step. A small one, but it counted nonetheless, and I was proud of her. She also stepped up at work, standing up for a well-deserved higher salary. Then there was deciding to change her stylist. After an appointment that I paid for and she was unhappy with—with her pretty much grey-dyed hair, Mel debated on getting a new hairstylist. She loved Natalie, but she just didn't seem to get Mel's wishes right. She also planned on eating healthy by going back to the 21-day fix plan. For once, she seemed to be getting her life under control and I felt hope that things may just work out.

Mel had me wrapped around her little finger. I had no idea what kind of a spell she had put on me, but most of the time, it was hard to stop thinking about her. When she was ready, I wanted to go down on her while she left something inside her. I promised to her that I wouldn't touch or even look and would instead just concentrate on the other area. I wanted to try everything and anything with her. More than anything else, I wanted to make her feel good.

I continued urging her to talk to me and open up more than ever. I wanted us both to progress further and be the best versions of ourselves.

Mel scored four tickets and a parking pass for Sunday night's hockey game. Her disagreement with Kelly was long forgotten by now, so she said she'd ask Kelly and Steve to go with us. I agreed but insisted that she comes to the hunting expo with me. It only seemed fair. Mel promised that she'd come along.

Come Christmas, we had big plans. There was a Christmas party at Mel's workplace; I asked her if she wanted me to come along and she said no; she would have rather had me stay at home and take care of the dog. She wasn't intending on staying long anyway. Then there was the annual Christmas shopping—a long weekend ahead of us. Mel wanted me to come along; that much I could tell from how many times she had asked if I'd come along. I was happy to oblige, just as I was happy to pay for everything.

Intimately, regardless of what I was desperately trying to point out, Mel kept her sexual desires to herself again, often pleasuring herself after I'd fall asleep. I tried to convince her that she didn't need to wait for me to fall asleep—she could do anything, show me anything and tell me anything. I wanted to throw in some new toys. Cuffs, perhaps, because she definitely needed to be disciplined with the way that she teased me.

Mel was forced to take a step back due to her reoccurring UTIs, but she would still keep a track of my movements. She even suggested that we keep journals, which was something she said a psychiatrist was going to suggest anyway. She was certain that once she got her UTI fixed and started getting on a healthier road, she would be so much happier and that would transfer onto me and her sexual desire for me. She was paralyzed with fear about UTIs and yeast infections, and she claimed that was the only reason why she was putting some distance in between us… But with time, she said, as we started eating better, exercising, and taking vitamins, our sex life would only be more intense. She was already there mentally, eager to explore all the possibilities, and she just needed to get there physically.

I assured her that I was on standby and ready to embrace whatever she dished out. Basically, with no boundaries, aside from no guys, of course. Mel and I seemed to be on the same page there, though. Another man in a threesome would be a huge turnoff for her, she said. I couldn't agree more. I would have never wanted to share her with another man. But little did I know…

Mel wasn't feeling too well in general, and I figured it was just a lot of things adding up. Stress, lack of sunlight, and daylight hours. There was also a lack of an actual vacation, holidays… Our work, what we ate and drank, and lastly, our new nightlife had put some stress on us as we worked everything out. She was hopeful about the new year. New year, new goals, better lifestyle, she said. On top of that, she also wanted a new puppy. I would have given her anything she asked for, so I agreed under one condition—there had to be a kennel. I wanted no destruction in our house.

Four days before Christmas, Mel went to her sister's place, giving me some time on my own. I knew what needed to be done during this time—now that she was away and I had my peace. I went to purchase a ring for her. A few weeks back, she excitedly asked me if we could go to the jewels because I had promised her a few days prior that we would. I agreed with her, telling her that we could, but only when she finally opened up to me. Regardless of my words, I decided to get her a present I knew would make her happy. I chose one that I thought would suit her, and I was certain that she would like it too.

And it did make her happy. She thought that the ring was the most beautiful thing, and she couldn't thank me enough for taking care of her and her dog and fostering her dreams. She continued to say that I was the best thing that had ever happened to her.

We spent an incredible Christmas together that year, even if we knew that money was going to get a little tight afterward—at least for Mel. There was Rosey's vet appointment that was going to cost a lot, but Mel was optimistic about 2020. She was also down to 138.8 pounds and couldn't wait to start the 21-day fix program. Again, there was the promise that once she got her confidence back, it would help our sex life a lot. I loved her body just as it was, but I supposed that was something that didn't matter. She had to love herself first. I found her incredibly sexy and wouldn't have cared if she lost or gained another twenty-five pounds. All I wanted was to be close to her. Still, I supported her as I always did.

FIVE
A NEW YEAR (JANUARY 2020 - MARCH 2020)

New Year's Eve 2019. We stayed home and had some drinks. We watched the ball drop on TV and enjoyed the evening. Sometime just after midnight, we stumbled into bed and had sex, plain vanilla, but it was always good. Afterward, we lay there and talked for several minutes. Eventually, Mel got out of bed and headed to the bathroom, and I went out to the garage for a nightcap. I stopped in the half bath to relieve myself on the way out. While in the bathroom, I heard Mel run upstairs, then maybe 15 seconds later run back down. There were some things on the stairs that she knocked over on the way down, causing a loud noise. Still in the bathroom, I yelled out if she was ok, but I didn't hear anything. I washed my hands and went to check on her. As I walked into the bedroom, Mel was all wrapped up in bed and lying still. I asked if she was ok, and she said what? I said I heard you run upstairs and back down, knocking stuff over, and I was worried she was hurt. She replied that she didn't go upstairs. She was obviously lying, but I thought it must be her sex toy secret and backed off. I took care of my nightcap and went to sleep. I didn't set the audio recorder that night, but I should have. I should have stayed up longer. It wouldn't have mattered anyway. She would have just waited until I eventually fell asleep.

Mel would sleep in till almost noon on weekends which was odd because she went to bed at 8-9 p.m. the night before. I knew she wasn't sleeping, maybe half or less of that time. Mel took Monday and Tuesday off work that first week of the year and several other days during January and February. She also visited her sister a lot. We had our issues, but her dad once told me Mel was sickly and took many sick days, so I didn't think much of it.

After another pretzel session and rejection for sex, and was about to take care of myself when I asked Mel if I could hold her down there while I finished. Mel had the left side of the bed, but I'm ambidextrous, so it didn't matter to me. She agreed, and as I slid my hand under her pajamas and underwear, I felt something odd going up the crease of her leg. It was like a thinly weaved cord with a small barrel on the end. I checked the other side, and there was one there too. I slowly followed where they went, and they headed down further. But Mel kept her legs held shut, so I could not reach. Then I pulled my hand back up, grabbed one of the barrels, and gave a slight pull. She immediately pulled my hand away and asked what I was doing. I asked her what that was, and she said it must be part of her pajamas or something. I said no, it wasn't, and she told me to check. I tried, but she held her legs tight so I couldn't get in. I got frustrated, and she told me I could check again after she went to the bathroom. I didn't bother at that point, as we both got angry, and the mood was gone. That is when things started to go downhill. It was hard to handle the gaslighting, especially when she touched me with it. I had a hard time mentally dealing with this. Is it a game? Does she think everything will be ruined if she shows me? I wasn't sure what to think, but again, I thought it was not worth ending things over Mel's secret toy usage. When we argued about these things, she would hold back and would not touch me for a couple of days. I wrote her a letter one day out of frustration:

The thing that doesn't exist

I don't mind you having it, but you should use it "with" me. Not lying next to me (or sitting next to me). Especially after rejecting me. Apparently, you have no idea how much it hurts. Give the ring to the thing that doesn't exist because that is what you are married to. Don't patronize me anymore, don't call me crazy anymore, and don't have guilt or pity sex with me anymore. You are pushing me away.

Mel responded that I needed help. She still claimed that I was feeling and hearing things that didn't exist, and all she was doing was sleeping. She said I was hallucinating, blamed it on weed, and wanted me to quit and seek therapy. We argued, and I was cut off for a few days. She still did everything whenever I was cut off while lying next to me. Sometimes I would shake my foot to cover the vibration until I fell asleep. Mel would then complain about me shaking the bed, so I asked her to wait a few minutes until I fell asleep, but she just denied doing anything. On those nights, I usually ended up on the couch or upstairs. I kept going back for more, but I told her she must open up and share more to move forward. I was also getting very suspicious that this was more than a game. I wasn't getting any answers from her, so I looked at her external hard drive for anything I could find. I saw some sexually related memes she shared with her ex. Not much of a big deal, but she treated me differently. I chalked it up to a new thing and kept looking. No info about her nightly games, but I thought someone must know about this. That is when I remembered three words that someone once said to me. They told me to "watch her sleep." but I couldn't remember who told me this. I assumed it was her ex, Todd, who called me the first night she returned and left the voice mail years ago. Maybe that's why he kicked her out. Perhaps he found out about what she does at night and had enough. Did he try to warn me? I didn't want to contact him.

This haunted me for well over a year before I finally remembered. The mind is amazing. If it wants to forget something, it does. Trying to recall a deleted memory is difficult.

Maybe a year prior, Mel had mentioned that her ex, Todd met someone else, had a couple of kids, and was getting married. She sounded upset or jealous when she told me. Maybe it was because he was getting married before we were, or was it something more? For some reason, Mel liked to creep on her exes. I always told her that was unhealthy, and she shouldn't be doing that—another red flag.

At the start of the new year, I told her I would go to see a therapist. Mainly to tell my story and maybe understand why Mel is not telling me the truth. I made an appointment and started going. She wanted to go with me, but I told her to let me see him alone first. She was very upset about that. In the very first session, I described what I was going through. What I felt, heard, and saw. He told me I am 99.9 percent not crazy and asked me if Mel had any trauma in the past. Not that I was aware of, but I told him I would ask. He suggested we look at toys and buy something together. I told him I had tried before, and she refused anything that went inside. He said to try to pick out something like what I thought she was using. He felt that she might feel guilty about using toys we didn't buy together. So, a couple of days later, I tried one evening again while we were sitting on the couch. We brought the laptop out, and I searched for something like what I thought she was using and wanted to see her reaction. I think I found something similar. I tried. I really tried. She again shot down everything and said nothing that goes inside. I didn't know what else to try. She continually claimed to be doing nothing but sleeping, so we didn't get anything. I asked her if she had ever had any childhood trauma. She said there was a time when she was fourteen and the family went on vacation and her older sister's boyfriend, Steve, went with them. They had two conjoined hotel rooms. The parents stayed in one and Mel, Kelly, and Steve in the other. Mel said one day, Steve came out of the shower with just a towel on and asked Mel if she had ever seen a penis. Mel said no, so Steve asked her if she wanted to see one. She told me Steve showed her, but nothing else happened. I asked her if Kelly knew about this. At first, Mel said Kelly was in the room but then said she wasn't. I felt there was more to the story, but that was all Mel would say. I think she wanted to change the subject because Mel said, "What about other people?" I was not expecting that, but I went along, and we discussed it. I don't remember much of the conversation, probably because I assumed it was just fantasy and nothing would come of it. I do remember saying how it could not be anyone we knew. Burner phones and hotels were mentioned, along with fake names and certain online sites. I asked if she ever had a threesome, and she replied yes, with her recent ex Todd and her slutty friend Carrie. She said they had a few drinks and were in a hot tub but didn't want to talk about it. I thought that must be why Mel was upset and thought Carrie would go after Todd back when they broke up, but who knows. Mel once told me that she thought the owner of the hair salon she goes to was hot, so I asked about her. Mel said she didn't believe it was a good idea because the owner's ex was a heroin addict. And it was probably best to stay away from toxic people (little did I know). Towards the end of the conversation, I mentioned that this "other people" thing never works out. One always sneaks behind the other's back, and everything falls apart. We didn't talk about it after that, so I assumed it was the end of that idea.

Over the next week, things remained quiet, but nothing changed. It didn't take long for another argument about the gaslighting. Afterward, Mel said she needed a break and would stay the night at her sister's that Friday. I never objected to her going anywhere, so I told her to have fun and be careful. On Saturday morning, I was making the bed and noticed the fitted sheet was extremely worn on Mel's side of the bed. It was like the material was rubbed away and was almost see-through. Very similar to Mel's underwear. I knew the sheets were less than a year old, and my side was fine. I assumed it had to be from her all-night toy play and was caused by wedging a vibrator up against the sheet for hands-free use. Or maybe her elbow? I really had no idea, but that's what I told myself. Mel came home Saturday evening, and we were back at it that night. The next day, I noticed the sheets were worse and starting to tear. I asked Mel about it, but she claimed it was from night sweats. Since when does sweat wear material off? I didn't buy her excuse, but I thought it was somehow from her excessive secret toy use and let it go.

Then on Monday morning, as I was leaving for work, I noticed our trash cans were knocked over. There was a dusting of fresh snow on the ground, so when I got out to pick them up, I could see the tire tracks. They slowly ran into them, then carefully pulled away. The tread pattern was clear with no sliding, so whoever it was, did it on purpose. When I told Mel about it, she gave excuses like someone must have slid into them, which had happened to her before. I told her there were no sliding marks, so it was on purpose. We figured maybe the neighbor did it and dropped it.

Meanwhile, Mel kept pushing to go to the therapist with me, and I thought it was time she went too. The following was the email I sent him on 01/21/2020:

Hi Walter,

After talking with Mel last night, she said she wants to attend Monday's (01/27/2020) session at 4 p.m. with us

*(unless you have something sooner). Would that be ok?
She still swears nothing is going on, and something is
wrong with me. So, if you are ok with having her come
in Monday (or sooner), I would suggest the meeting be
about how I'm delusional and how to fix whatever is
spurring my hallucinations. I will go along with
anything to make our relationship better. Please let me
know. Thank you.*

His response was:

I understand. She is welcome to attend. Excellent.

Monday came, and I met Mel at Walter's office after work. It was awkward, but I knew that was going to happen. Mel talked about my obsession with sex and how she doesn't need it all the time. Walter was understanding but also mentioned that sex is an important part of a relationship. At some point, Mel blurted out, "I hate sex!" It was odd because she just threw it out there. She continued and said it was painful. The therapist didn't know what to say. I did, but I didn't want to argue in front of the therapist. She never experienced pain when we had sex. It was always good and enjoyable. The only time I remember her feeling pain was during the occasional doggie. Sometimes, if I missed my timing and things went on too long, it became uncomfortable for her, which was rare but has happened. We also talked about the vibrations and pretzeling. They said what I feel and hear is not real. What I saw Mel doing under the blankets was an interpretation of my mind wanting her to do those things. All delusions. I suppose I asked for it when I told him to side with her to avoid arguments. Walter then suggested that I tell Mel whenever I felt any vibrations and to throw the blankets off and look for whatever it was. I told him I tried that, but it never worked because of how many layers and her heavy weighted blanket. She always has time to hide things. Besides, whenever I did that, it certainly ruined the moment. I explained that whatever it was, was in her at times, so they both agreed for me to do a cavity check. That felt wrong and made me very uncomfortable, so I was against it. Mel then got angry and said I didn't want to check because I was afraid of finding nothing. Because if I found nothing, it would mean I'm truly delusional and would end my fantasy of her being a sexual deviant. Mel had no problems with it and encouraged me to check. She claimed to want this to end as well. She said she loved me and would do anything for us. Ok, so that was the task they came up with for me.

For the next few evenings, Mel didn't use the vibrators with me, only her hands. Then she started again, but I held back because I wanted the attention. I enjoyed it, but I knew it would end when I told her I felt something. They were times she touched me and would ask if I felt anything, and I would say no, so she wouldn't stop. I felt bad for lying, but I liked it too. I also desperately wanted it to lead to more and hoped she would eventually open up and tell me. A few nights later, we started our pretzel session, but I was tired and wasn't much into it, so I thought I should try the cavity check. I waited until I could tell it was in her. Then I told her I felt the vibrations and would do a cavity check. She encouraged me and I started peeling the layers of bedding off. Then she pushed her pajamas down and said ok. Her motions didn't seem natural, but I didn't know any better. When I reached down to check, Mel held her legs shut tight, and I had to ask her to open a little. She did slightly, and I slid a finger inside. I noticed something odd right away. Her cervix was right there, like an inch or so in. At the time, I didn't know what that meant. Only later did I figure out that she must have pushed the toy out, and I should have checked underneath her. It was a shameful experience, and I told myself I wouldn't do that again. She had no issues with it and encouraged me to check whenever I felt something. I knew she was mocking me at that point, and I didn't understand how to catch her. I was beyond frustrated. I researched how they check in women's prisons, and I guess they lay a mirror down and have them squat on top of it while forcefully coughing. Maybe that would have worked, but I didn't want to depend on the person gaslighting me to prove my sanity. I wanted to find out without her knowing and decided to order a mini-spy camera. Something small I could hold and maybe get my hand close enough to record something under the blankets. After receiving the camera, I charged it up and was ready to use it. I got in bed that night and, of course, pretzeled. I got the camera going and moved my hand into position when she must have noticed something. She said, "What's in your hand?" I quickly pulled it away and said nothing. "What's in your hand!?" She yelled and threatened to leave if I was lying to her, but I calmed her down and convinced her it was nothing. Needless to say, the camera didn't work out. I also tried setting the camera up in a bin of dog toys next to her side of the bed, but when left on motion-activated recording, the battery only lasted 45 minutes. Again, not good enough. Being a new house, with very little junk lying around, there were no places to conceal a camera. I thought about one of those smoke detector cameras, but they didn't have good reviews, and not to mention it needed wi-fi which we didn't have. I didn't have many options. I had another plan I would try. Sometimes after pretzeling, she would turn over and face me. Usually when she had enough of me, but sometimes not. Sometimes she would slowly slide her hand under the blankets and touch me with the vibrating thing as long as I didn't move my hands towards her. If I did, she would quickly pull her hand back. I wanted to be touched, so I kept my hands still. Now that I had the camera, I thought I would try again, and I would for sure be able to record it. I tried, and several times I thought I was successful and went to sleep thinking I had her. The next morning after Mel would leave for work; I would review the footage only to find she again was a step ahead of me. She stayed on the other side of a sheet, and all I could see was the sheet moving closer until it touched me. Thoroughly disappointed, I ended up giving up on the camera. I still had the recording app on my phone and started to record more even though I told her I wouldn't anymore. But I needed to know. I hid the notification that it was running on my phone because she had checked a few times. I noticed that she would continue her routine then I heard what I believed to be unplugging her phone and watching porn. She turned the volume down, but I still heard some slapping sounds and an occasional female moan (which wasn't Mel, she was quiet). I could tell she was still in bed, and it wasn't a big deal to watch porn or masturbate. I thought it was hot. Then there were nights she started to leave the room after I fell asleep. I assumed it was to watch porn in the other room with her laptop. During those times, I could hear very little. Usually, faint slapping noises, but one recording had a couple of female whimpers (not Mel). But I expected to hear those noises because I thought she was watching porn. Other than that, just noises of walking around and doors opening and closing. I assumed the doors were the pantry and refrigerator. Mel would also let the dog out a couple of times out the sliding door during the night. A few times, the dog barked and growled, and Mel would say out loud, "that's just deer," to the dog, so that's what I assumed it was. I didn't use the audio recorder every night as it sucked taking the time to listen to them. I probably should have, though.

One morning, I heard a zipper opening and closing as I woke up. I assumed that is where Mel was putting the things that do not exist. I made a mental note to try and catch it the next morning. The next morning came, and after she got up, I tried to look without Mel noticing. She went to her dresser, opened a drawer, and pulled out a small black bag with a white floral pattern. She opened it up, quickly shoved a couple of things into it, and immediately left the room with it. I thought about jumping up and demanding to see what was in the bag, but then I thought that would create a bad situation, and I wanted to be closer to her and understand her, not push her away. I still wanted to figure things out by myself without her knowing. At the time, I only wanted to see the toys she was using. That was it. I assumed if she thought I still didn't know what she was using, everything would be ok. Maybe I should have jumped up because, as it turns out, I never saw them. There are many things I didn't do or should have done differently. What happened next is a prime example. It was a Saturday night near the end of February. After another pretzel session, I went to the garage for a nightcap. It was 3 a.m., and I was groggy. I was getting ready to come back in when I thought I heard a vehicle slowly pulling into the end of the driveway. There were larger stones on the side of the driveway, near the street, and driving over these larger rounded rocks made a distinct noise. I didn't hear them pull back out or any doors open or close. I thought it could be someone pulling in the neighbors' across the street, but I didn't remember him having large stones in his driveway. It was 3 a.m.; I had just smoked a little weed and was a minute or two from passing out. I had no reason to think Mel had anything going on except for the toy usage, so my next thought was the doors are locked, I have guns, and I didn't check and went back to bed. I did turn on the audio recorder that night, though. The next day we went grocery shopping, and on the way there, she mentioned something about not liking the weed I had in the garage. I asked how she knew, and Mel said she had trouble sleeping the night before and wanted to see if that helped because it seemed to work for me. I told her it looked like someone was in my weed drawer, so maybe she was covering before I had the chance to say anything. It wasn't a big deal, though. I've told her that it helped me sleep and was probably better than prescriptions. But she always said she never liked it, so I was surprised she tried some. I didn't think it was a big deal until I listened to the audio later. What I heard on the audio had me concerned. Sometime after I went to sleep, she got up, left the room, and quietly shut the bedroom door behind her. She walked across the house and opened the squeaky garage door. I had no idea what happened after that or when she came back inside. Eventually, she returned to bed, but I had no idea of the time because there were no time stamps on the recording. At the time, I had no reason to suspect anyone else of being involved, so I had a hard time processing what happened. I told Mel what I heard in the garage and asked if she knew who pulled into the driveway last night? Her reply was, "no one," and that I was being paranoid. I thought that was an odd answer, and it took me a couple of weeks to figure out why. At first, I thought maybe someone was delivering drugs to her. After all, I knew she was addicted to opiates. Then I thought, no drug dealer is going to deliver at 3 a.m. unless something else was involved. So, I decided to ask Mel about that night again, beginning with, do you remember that night you smoked some weed to help you sleep? And she replied that she doesn't smoke weed and never went out to the garage that night or any night to smoke weed. I was confused because she just gave her excuse of going out to the garage on the recording, which she didn't know I had. I didn't want Mel to know I was recording again, so I kept that to myself. Then I asked her again who pulled in the driveway that night? Her answer was again, "No one. It's all in your head," she sternly claimed. But I knew she was lying because if she were sleeping, the correct answer would have been, "How should I know? I was sleeping." I didn't say anything and wanted to see how long it took until she realized what she was saying. She kept telling me she wasn't doing anything wrong and blamed weed for our problems. I tried not smoking a few times before bed, but nothing changed. We continued to argue, and a few times, she threw the audio file of her masturbating in my face, claiming there was nothing there either. She knew I deleted them. Frustrated, I downloaded some file recovery software and tried to retrieve the deleted audio files. I didn't have any luck, so I went to my tech-savvy brother's house to help, which Mel didn't like, but to no avail. Unfortunately for me, the recovered files were corrupted and impossible to repair.

With no proof of anything and her continued denial, I thought it best to forget and continue living. I started designing a deck for the house, and Mel picked out seeds for the garden and landscaping flowers. She also cross-stitched a lot. On date nights, we did puzzles and drank wine. To help with the number of rejections, I devised some "rules of engagement." If she wanted to pretzel, the result would be 50% PIVY, 25% BJ, 25% HJ or myself. I knew that wasn't going to happen, but I tried. Mel said she was receptive to the idea, but her actions never changed. I continued having hope for us, but looking back, it was just wishful thinking.

About this time, the covid scare was starting, so we decided it was probably best to cancel our wedding in August. Two other couples we knew also postponed their wedding. Besides, the way things were going, we weren't going to make it.

JANUARY 2020 – MARCH 2020

New year, new us.

Or at least that was what the all New Year cliche sayings said. Mel was determined to get thin, pulling out old photos of herself for inspiration. One, in particular, was a photo of her with her favorite earrings that she wore when we went hunting one time, and I told her to take them off. She did, but they rusted in her hunting jacket. She still kept them there. That photo represented a dark time in my life, but I looked forward to a great future with her and being the happiest and greatest we can possibly be. Mel found it funny that it was a dark time in my life because she was conflicted about it herself. On the one hand, it was the time when I started texting her again, but she was hurting inside watching her mother die. She said that she was the happiest with me, right here and right now.

"Always forward, never back," she said.

I was glad I reached out to her when I did. I was also glad her mother got to know that I was with her, treating her well and giving her the happiest life I possibly could. Mel said that her mother has seen it all along and was with us all the time. I could only hope so. I hoped that she was proud of how we were turning out. We still needed a little work, but not much.

I tried to be fair with Mel. I didn't want her to do anything if her first thought was no. I told her that if she didn't want me, she didn't have to do anything—in fact, I urged her not to. It hurt me so much to know that she was only doing certain things to please her, and I promised both to myself and her that I wouldn't push anymore. It shouldn't have been so hard to approach me, and I needed to wait for her to want me. Until then, I would continue to do my best and love her like she deserved to. Mel again pointed out that she was struggling with work, but was trying her best. I hoped she would get past whatever work stuff was bothering her. It was hard not to take work stress home, if not impossible—I knew that better than anyone else… But I offered to be there for her and take her mind away if she wanted me to. I could tell something was really bothering her, and I hoped that it was only work. Either way, I was there for her. Mel assured me it was just work and told me she had come up with a plan that she would show to me. She even put dates to everything to keep herself on track.

I was desperate to understand her so these bad thoughts I had could go away, but things in general seemed to take a turn for the worse. Mel struggled at work again—they gave her some bullshit answer about how she made enough money for her job code. When she asked them to provide her with that information, her superior said she couldn't send it directly to Mel but could set up a call to discuss it. Mel was more than discouraged with work, and then there were our own struggles. She thought it would be best if she disappeared.

I tried to explain myself. I didn't think she didn't desire me anymore, I just thought she preferred and was possibly addicted to something else as far as our sex life went. I was actually not sure, because she didn't talk to me about this stuff other than to say I was delusional. Without her talking to me, I felt lost, confused, and hurt. Her place on earth with me and our animals meant more than just a sexual preference and satisfaction, or her job. She needed to be happy, and we needed to be happy. Happiness was up to us, and more than anything else, I wanted to make it happen.

Mel debated me on this, telling me that there was nothing she was addicted to, nor did she masturbate or have any device that she used at night. If she did, she would have shared it with me because she was sick of this back and forth between us. She said she was scared to even sleep next to me now because of it. She was hurt by my words but said she would take a lie detector or sleep naked with no blankets to prove to me that she was not doing what I thought. I had nothing to hide, she claimed. I was the problem, apparently, constantly checking on her, looking at her phone, wondering what she was doing at every moment and letting my thoughts run wild. All she wanted was to be happy. She didn't think I wanted to resolve the issue; we were just going to co-exist until I decided I would either go get professional help with her, or come with her to take a lie detector test.

She was wrong. I desperately wanted to solve this issue. I hadn't found any lie-detector reviews that were good, and it probably wasn't the proper way to clear things up anyway. Mel said she would agree to anything just to put this chapter behind us, once and for all. There were only three places on the area. One place wasn't accepting new patients, second place was all set to make an appointment, but I wanted to talk to her first. They charged $150 per one session or $500 for four. Unless, of course, we managed to find a way to figure this out on our own.

Mel still swore she was upfront and honest about everything with me. It bothered me that I couldn't make her feel safe enough to tell me about her sexuality and her preferences.

"When was the last time you used a vibrating device on yourself?" I asked her.

"I don't know the exact date, but I know with certainty since this has become an issue, I have not used it," she said. She also said there has been so much emphasis on sex that she didn't even want to think about it because it caused this horrible rift between us. That only upset me more. She either had selective memory or didn't want us to be together. I couldn't help but wonder if she was actually trying to find a reason to leave, because something like this shouldn't even have been an issue. The only issue was that she was not honest with me about this stuff.

Mel warned me to tell her if I wanted to leave. She said I claimed to love her, no matter what, but when I was honest and real with her, I would call her a liar. She could no longer take it, and there was nothing she could do about it. She said I was obsessed with sex and that this whole issue of ours began back in August.

"Write down a list of questions and I'll take a lie detector test," she told me. "If you don't believe me, that's on you. Not me. I'm sick and tired of not being enough for you. Unless I have sex with you, you go ballistic on me enough to throw your ring at me." She felt as if I was throwing her out the door, and it was all apparent to her now.

I loved her no matter what, even when I knew she would take this to her grave and let it ruin us.

"By the way, I owe you a vibrating razor as the one I looked at this morning was just used and has fresh blood coming out of the crevices…" I told her after she had continuously tried to convince me otherwise. "You see, it's not me that needs to be honest. Maybe a female broke into our house and used it—while on her period—in the last couple of days?"

I just wanted her to be honest with me and things would be okay… But if she continued to lie, they wouldn't be. I wasn't even sure why she subconsciously wanted to sabotage our relationship. We had such a beautiful thing going and this kept happening. I no longer wanted to talk to her about it, because all she did was lie to me. It broke my heart and absolutely crushed me, and I was determined to sleep upstairs until this was solved. For me, it wasn't sex with me or sex with her. It was sex together. It wasn't supposed to be a chore or a duty, but a mutually pleasurable act of pure love.

"You need help," she responded. "I have not used it, especially on my period. Are you serious? That is so fucking gross." Again, with the lies. She used it but said it was gross. "How about I shoot myself tonight? Then you can see what's more important to you… Us, or your guns. You will get enough money to not worry about this anymore, and I will be saved from a life of never living up to what you want. I've hit that point."

"No, please don't do that," I begged her. I was terrified of losing her, and the world momentarily stopped spinning for me. I just wanted us to be okay. "You are my world and the animals, and I will be lost. We must get this figured out without fighting."

Later that day, we had a long talk, and I settled on starting to see a therapist. I had my first session soon—I told her that she could come along, but perhaps not for the first session. If she did want to join (which I assumed she would), she could be added as a note on mine, but if she wanted a session by herself, it would have to go through her insurance—that was what they told me.

"Whatever you want me to do, I will be happy to do. We are tackling this," she told me.

The vibrations were present again. They would appear every so often during the night, and I could never figure out where they came from. They affected my sleep, and I'd often have a hard time during the night. I felt bad that I was having issues, but I was determined to solve them. Mel would stay up much of the night to make sure I was okay, monitoring me and making sure I slept well once I did manage to fall asleep.

She was determined to quit her job; she wasn't even sure she could give it two weeks. She didn't want to train anyone; if the company didn't care about her, why should she care about them? They thought a co-op could do what she did, so she would let them just figure it out on their own. The place would go up in flames if she was to just walk out. There were so many things she needed to do, she couldn't even put them into a list. She made the decision to spend some time on Sunday updating her resume and getting it posted, and updating her LinkedIn. It was finally time for her to leave that place that sucked the life out of her.

"Sticking to my goal list I made," she told me. She had a degree, and eight years of corporate experience, seven of which had been in a finance role. She was proficient in Microsoft Excel and could do circles around anyone when it came to being detail-oriented. I supported her decision. As always, I just wanted her happy.

Along with her work, my nights were getting tougher, too. I often hoped she would have her restless leg syndrome later during the night. I knew that sounded bad, but that seemed to be the only time I didn't hear or feel anything. Mel couldn't figure out what was causing it, either, but she hoped we could make love and not have a big blow-up like we usually did.

The two of us put our sex life on pause for a little while until we figured things out. I missed connecting with her, but I knew it was for the best. The vibrations continued, leaving me confused, but I would do my best to take care of myself and fall asleep. Whatever it was, I hoped it would be fixed soon.

Mel could feel things weren't right, too. She told me she couldn't continue to be the brunt of my bad days.

"It seems like when you don't want to do something, like go to my dad's for a birthday celebration, or whatever the occasion is, you take it out on me or whomever we're around. It's not fair. You have done it quite a few times in the last three months. I don't deserve to continue getting hurt by your attitude. I'm not doing anything wrong or anything to hurt you… So I can't understand why you would do that to me or the people we're around," she told me. "I need a break from everything and after the hunting expo this Saturday, I'm taking the dog and staying the night at Kelly's." As she had promised, she would come to the hunting expo with me this Saturday. She even rescheduled the dog grooming appointment to be able to do it.

I didn't mean to act malicious toward her, and it wasn't what she thought. Those days happen after I experienced the vibrations, and usually left me confused and hurt. Not because I didn't want to do these things with her... But because I wanted to do them with her. Everything had definitely taken its toll on me, but hopefully, I would be able to learn to deal with it by talking to someone.

Mel hoped therapy would help. She said I had been taking my frustrations out on her every weekend since before Thanksgiving. Her family noticed it, too, and that made it that much worse.

It was just how I was wired. When I was hurting, my attitude reflected. I had to get over this and learn how to accept the way things are. Life was short so I had to learn to accept the things I couldn't change. Through therapy, I hoped to get some tips on how to do just that.

I would often try to prepare what we would do during our night time during the day. I'd flirt, and jokingly suggest different positions, and Mel would usually leave me hanging, saying that she wasn't a big fan of doing this at 11:30 or midnight every night. I hoped we could come to some kind of a compromise because she really turned me on. Even after all these years we had spent together, she turned me on as no other person has ever done. We were still sleeping separately, giving each other time to miss one another, but I would occasionally put some of her perfume on her pillow to sleep easier. It seemed to help.

Finally, I sent the psychologist an email asking if Mel could attend Monday's session, if not a sooner session. The vibrations were louder and more prominent. Mel swore once again she didn't know where they were coming from—she swore on her dog's life that she was telling me the truth. She also offered once again to take a lie detector test.

"You can write down all the questions you want, and I have no problem answering them. I surely hope we can get to the bottom of all of this. I would *never* hide anything from you," she told me. And I trusted her.

Mel was increasingly getting more and more worried about me, urging me to find a primary care doctor and make an appointment. She said I needed a physical and a mental health screening and was terrified of losing me. I assured her I was fine, telling her I'd look into it during lunch and call my therapist.

Aside from therapy, I also made an active effort to be the happiest we could be. Mel wanted to figure out a way to make our vegetables and fruits last all year long. Not just summer. She wanted to get better at canning and preserving, but it was something that took a shit ton of time that she didn't have. I told her that with all the work we did, it was important that we took some time for ourselves, too. That included gardening. I didn't want us to fall into a groove of never having any time to do other things. We hadn't even taken the kayaks out or went to the camp last year. I didn't want that to happen anymore. I also came up with the idea to come up with "rules of engagement" when being intimate. I thought it would be fun, and I could only hope she'd feel the same way, too. For example, the results of pretzeling should be: 50% pivy, 25% blowjob and 25% I took care of myself or nothing. She agreed, but told me not to expect much if I got home at 8:00 p.m.

Mel was trying to stick it out at work, still. There was a bonus in the play—a bonus that we desperately needed to get our finances in order. She promised herself she wouldn't quit until she got that bonus. She wished they would have laid her off, but she was doing her best to stay calm, even when they asked her about stuff from 2014 (which should have clearly been written off already). I encouraged her to ignore it and try not to let it get to her.

It didn't help that her doctor started weaning her off meds. She knew it was coming and was okay with it. It meant kratom and working out would be the norm now.

Oddly enough, we seemed to be closer, so I would snap photos of her here and there to keep in my gallery. Mel didn't like me taking photos and videos of her without her knowing (unless her butt looked good in it). I encouraged her to pose for me. No one turned me on like her. I was forgiven for the occasional photos, because I took care of her in every way, as she said.

"No one else has ever come close to doing for me what you have. I've been with you for eight years and they haven't always been easy, but I wouldn't want to do life with anyone else, babe. You are my everything. You are smart, good-looking, sexy, thoughtful, fuck smart... You're the most intelligent man I know, and we make a great team," she texted me one morning. It made my heart happy to hear her appreciate my efforts to always be there for her and take care of her.

After Valentine's Day, Mel was fuming. Turning in her ring had become an ordeal. She decided she may not be getting it done if they continued to give her crap about inspecting the diamonds and not covering the cost of it. She was upset because they didn't know whether they could size it down, but we figured we would sort it out somehow. My birthday was coming up, too, and she asked me what I wanted as my birthday present.

"Bucket teeth for tractor," I told her. "And... Or vibrations."

Come next hunting expo, I was excited to go with Mel... But it seemed that there was a misunderstanding. She thought that we settled on not going and made plans with Kelly, telling me to go and that she would certainly come to the next one. The other night when we spoke about it, she told me she was concerned about being on her feet for six hours—which I didn't think meant that it was determined that we weren't going.

"It'll be okay. I'll think about going by myself. I might not go now either..." I told her.

"Do you want me to cancel with Kelly and go with you? I have no problem doing that if your heart is really set on going," she responded.

"I have to think about it. I'm flustered and busy." Right now, I just didn't have the capacity to think about it.

Mel continued struggling with her medication and the endless circle of helping out Kelly by giving out her Ambien, and then being stuck without it later. Kelly would often come around telling her that she can't get any, and Mel would then retort that if she had known that she wouldn't have given her so many. She was upset that no one (except me) was helping her out, so why should she help others out? For God knows what time, she was done with everything and everyone—aside from us.

SIX

PURSUIT OF TRUTH? (MARCH 2020 - AUGUST 2020)

I COULDN'T STOP THINKING about the 3 am car that pulled into the driveway. My gut and head told me something was wrong, but my heart wanted solid proof. I needed to know. I decided to snoop on her laptop one day. I didn't know what I was looking for, but maybe something was there. I looked at internet history, nothing there but the vibrators we previously looked at and many Facebook visits. So I checked to see if it would automatically load her Facebook page. It didn't, but it took me to a page to choose which account to log into. The page showed the recent log-in accounts. One was Mel's, and the other had the name of Jennifer Something. I clicked on Jennifer and typed in one of Mel's common passwords. First try, and I was in. I quickly browsed around, not knowing where to look or what I would find. It was a blank profile with no pictures, posts, or friends. No liked pages or following anyone, nothing. I did happen to stumble upon a page that showed people she viewed. There were at least a dozen guys. I didn't recognize any of them except for two; they were her known exes she had previously told me about. One was Todd, and the other was an ex from long ago. I didn't take a picture of that screen but should have. There was probably more information, but I didn't know where to look. I checked messages and didn't see any, but I didn't check deleted messages. I'm not used to doing anything like this, so I'm sure I missed something. Ultimately, no proof.

Seeing her recent ex, Todd, on that list compelled me to do a little research to see what was going on in his life. Because he was the first person I thought might have pulled into the driveway. Mel had previously told me Todd got married and had a couple of kids. But I found out he filed for divorce in September when this whole thing started, and it was finalized right around the 3 a.m. driveway incident. Coincidence? That bothered me, and even though I knew it was wrong, I contacted Todd. He seemed too nice. I asked if he remembered what he left on my voicemail years prior, but he said he didn't. I asked if he told me to "watch her sleep"? To see if that rang a bell, but he didn't remember saying that. Then I asked if he noticed her doing anything weird at night, but he didn't remember Mel doing anything. Todd referred to her as "repulsive" and told me to check her phone if I thought she was doing something. He then invited me over for a beer so we could talk. I politely declined and thanked him for his time. I figured he was lying, so another dead end. I thought it might be better to contact his recent ex. Maybe she busted him cheating with Mel, and I was the only one who didn't know. Again, I knew it wasn't the right thing to do, but I felt like I was losing my mind. So, I contacted her, and she was nice. She told me she divorced Todd because she found out he was cheating but with a girl that had a Mexican name. She also mentioned that he wanted her to have a threesome with her (sound familiar?) Ok, not much info there. After hanging up, I remembered Mel worked with a younger female with whom she was close. It was the same last name, so I figured maybe Mel used a fake name to protect herself in case she was caught. Who knows? I forgot what she told me the first name was, so I contacted her again to ask, but she got angry and told me not to contact her again. I said no problem. I didn't get any solid info, just more suspicious circumstances. The next thing I know, I get an angry message from Todd for talking to his ex. No worries, I was done with them.

Now the phone. I had to be sneaky about it. Mel always told me I was free to look at her phone, but only in front of her. Besides, I was only interested in the deleted data, which you cannot see without recovery software. I cannot remember the exact process, but I remember downloading an app on my computer and grabbing her phone while she was actually sleeping. I cannot believe I got away with it. Scanning a phone can take a couple of hours, and it did. It finished and surprisingly I was able to put the phone back. Now I had the scan file on my computer and could preview all files but couldn't download them unless I hooked her phone back up. I looked at the files the next chance I got. I searched for images and sorted them by date. There were about thirty thousand images, which was a long and slow process. I found a bunch of sexually related memes not shared with me and cheating memes. Also, a breakup meme: "Sorry I dropped you, stop giving me that look" with a picture of a plastic milk jug that was dented and looked like a sad face. Other than that, I saw images of random people and a family, also random house pictures, random doors, entrances, and a couple of hallway pictures. Odd pics of our house too, with one from our bed to the doorway, then across the house from the couch to the kitchen door, garage door entrance to the kitchen, and kitchen entrance showing our island stools. Most were taken from a low perspective, as if from waist level. I didn't understand those pics at the time. I took pics of the preview images that I didn't understand. But I didn't find anything concrete.

Mel's phone contacts had a few questionable entries, but she later claimed they were old and carried over from the old phone. I know how that works, so that was believable. Next, I looked at the texts. When I reviewed the texts, nothing stuck out but a few odd things. First, I wanted to check the texts from Mel's slutty friend Carrie for obvious reasons, but they only went back a couple of months, and they were erratic, as if some were deleted right away and became unrecoverable. At least with the software, I was using. There was something else, though, and it took me a few minutes to figure it out. It was what I didn't see that triggered something. Mel used to share memes with Grump, who worked in the shop. I remember her telling me they shared memes because she forwarded one to me maybe eight months prior. I didn't think much of it, but looking back, I think they were mocking me. Grump was in a long-term relationship with this girl named Ann, and we were all friends on social media. Anyway, there was not a single text from him. She permanently deleted them all. I found that to be telling. I assumed the meme sharing took a wrong turn and got sexual until the point they acted on it. Then I remembered my work Christmas dinner when Grump was staring at Mel with his frowned face. Maybe that was when the "sorry I dropped you, stop giving me that look" meme was shared, along with some others that made sense. There was something odd about that night, but I didn't suspect anything at the time. I failed to pick up the signals right in front of me. That weekend Mel stayed at her sister's near Grump's place. She often stayed at her sister's, and I was beginning to put the pieces together. At one time, Mel, myself, and Grump all worked at the same place. When a foreign business bought out the company we worked for, management was dismantled, and a couple of the guys started their own business. They grew nicely and eventually hired my boss and a few others. A year later, I was forced out and went to work for them. Both Mel and Grump stayed. Flash forward maybe four years, and

Grump ended up getting fired. I remember Mel being worried for him and wondered if the company I worked at would hire him. Most of my coworkers knew him, so it wasn't surprising when Grump applied for a job. Management asked some employees if they thought he would make a good fit. They asked me, and I said sure, Grump appears to know what he's doing (everything seems to come back to haunt me). And he was hired.

When Mel first moved back to the area and started working with us, her dad told her to watch out for two guys. Me and Grump. Grump worked in the shop and was always unhappy and in a bad mood. I got along with him after I stood up to him because he was being a dick. Sometimes that's what it takes to get a simpleton's respect. Grump is an overweight, lazy drunkard whose seemingly only ambition was barely getting by and alcohol. He is a few years older than me and maybe six foot, two-fifty.

Along with the meme sharing, perhaps he was supplying Mel with drugs, which turned into something else. However, I had no proof—only circumstantial along with my gut feeling. One day, Grump came up to my cube and told me he and Ann decided to get a puppy and was going to pick it up near where Mel and I live. He asked for directions, which I thought was strange because everyone has GPS. He continued to stop by my cube to chat about meaning-less shit. Why the sudden small talk? I knew something had happened, and Mel was definitely hiding something. I thought for sure I would have found positive evidence on her phone. But where was it? I never saw any proof, but I wanted to gauge her reaction to those images I found. The next day, I asked Mel about looking at her phone, and she said sure and handed it to me. I walked over to the computer and plugged it in. She followed me and said, what are you doing? And I told her I wasn't interested in what was on her phone, only the deleted stuff. I'm glad I scanned it prior because it can take a couple of hours, and there was no way Mel would have let me do that. I opened the initial scan and showed her some images I found. Mel looked worried for a moment as her eyes widened, but that quickly changed to squinting and anger as she shouted where did you get those!? I told her from her phone, and she said she didn't know where those came from and immediately yanked her phone back.

It was mid-March when the lockdowns started. First, Mel got the call to stay home, then a week later, I got the call to stay home. Mel and I worked at home occasionally, so it wasn't a big deal for us. We never missed a day. We set up another office for her so she could work efficiently. But Mel slowed down and seemed depressed, which I think was due to several reasons. For one, after confronting Mel about the fake Facebook profile and looking at her phone, everything seemed to stop, or at least that is what I thought. For two, I was now working from home, so I was around more. Also, Mel said she quit taking her pain meds at the beginning of the month, or at least that is what she told me. She also kept telling me something was wrong with me and wanted me to get a physical. It had probably been twenty years since my last one, so I had no objections. I went, and when the results came back, everything was normal.

I ended up working at home for about three months. During that time, I had a hard time dealing with the 3 a.m. driveway occurrence and would try to stay up late all the time. Most nights, we still slept together and would on and off pretzel. Pivy remained hard to come by. On nights we argued, and I didn't feel like pretzeling; Mel continued by herself as she did every night. It bothered me, so I asked if she could stop and wait five minutes for me to fall asleep. She, of course, would deny doing anything, claim to be sleeping, and continue.

Frustrated, I would try shaking my foot to mask the vibrations. Sometimes it worked, and I fell asleep in a few minutes, and other times she would complain, then she or I would sleep on the couch or upstairs. On many occasions, I dreamt of building an EMP device to shut her down. The idea made me smile, but I never went through with it. Even when Mel would get up and sleep on the couch in the next room, I could still hear and feel vibrations and thought Mel was continuing to fuck with me. It was not a straight vibration; it was a repeating pattern. I thought maybe she turned something on and hid it under the mattress. I got out of bed and checked one time but didn't find anything. The DVR in our bedroom produced vibrations, so I moved it to the basement. The DVR had a different frequency that only lasted while it was updating or maybe recording a show, but I moved it anyway to eliminate a potential source. I thought perhaps I was becoming delusional. I told my therapist, and he said that I might have developed a hypersensitivity to vibrations because of how I was exposed to them. That still didn't explain where it came from, though. The vibrations were there every night, and I still thought Mel was fucking with me. I just learned to deal with it. She offered me Ambien on occasion, but I always refused. I thought she must have something planned and tried to stay up even longer. I always passed out, though. I have no idea if she ever slipped any to me. Possibly to lessen the chance of me waking up and catching her doing something or someone. She never needed to, though. I sleep like a rock. Sometimes during pretzel play, I would fall asleep if I was tired, and she ignored me for too long. I had asked her if I was responsive below after falling asleep.

I didn't know, but she said no. I thought it would be cool if it were. I thought that was funny, but other times I would wake up and feel sore but couldn't remember doing anything that made me sore. Mel would sometimes get a little aggressive, and a couple of times, I needed recovery time.

Since the Covid scare was still going on, Mel suggested we cancel our vacation and get a puppy. I agreed, but only if she took care of it. I would help, but the main responsibilities were hers. Our situation was rocky, but I was trying to keep us together. She claimed to want the same thing as well. Since we had a smaller dog, we decided to get a full-size farm dog. She found a breeder nearby and put in our deposit for a male in the next litter, which was coming soon. About a month goes by, and we are ready to visit with our new puppy. The breeder sent Mel pics, and we had already picked Ollie as a name for him. It seemed to fit. What I found strange was when we visited, the breeder told us she named him Sleepy. I looked at Mel and said, "Haa! He was meant for you." Mel heard me but didn't look at me. She hated the little jabs I gave her, but I thoroughly enjoyed them.

Eventually, my job called me back to the office. But Mel stayed working at home. I had a hard time because Grump worked in the shop. My gut feelings were making me sick. I took measures to avoid him, but he kept coming up to my cubicle, asking how the puppy was doing. I noticed he had bloodshot eyes like he only had a couple of hours of sleep. I wondered to myself if he was making long drives at night. I kept my answers short and acted busy so he would leave. I had no proof, so doing or saying anything would make me look like the bad guy. It felt like they were rubbing it in my face.

I struggled to go to work, but I quickly scheduled some vacation time as the material for the deck was expected to be delivered soon. Unfortunately, the delivery was late and maybe only thirty percent of the order. I was missing the material to get started but didn't want to go back to work. I talked with my boss and was able to extend my vacation time. The next week the remaining order came, but thirty percent was still missing. There was a lot of wrong material as well. It was a mess. I called and told them to return everything. I wasn't doing well mentally, which started affecting me physically. I was tired and broken. I lost about twenty pounds and felt weak. Before losing the weight, Mel and I would weigh ourselves often, and since the stuff started, I weighed 166.6 many times. It happened so often that I began to take pictures of the scale. Mel would jokingly call me the devil, but it didn't bother me. I'm not a superstitious person, but maybe there was something more behind it. Everything Mel accused me of, she was guilty of, so perhaps it makes sense.

With the deck fiasco over, I used my remaining vacation time to install security cameras covering all the exits. Mel wasn't happy about it but said she understood why I was doing it (Hmmm). She asked if there were any cameras on the inside, and I said no. Although, I should have installed one watching the power cords for the security camera DVR. I spent the next few days installing the cameras and setting them up. Mel told her family that I was paranoid and that "The weed" had got to my brain. I didn't care what anyone thought. I needed peace of mind, and only the truth was going to get me there. The system was flawed right from the start, though. It was for people trying to break into your home, not someone working on the inside. Mel could unplug/plug the system at her convenience. I looked to see if there was an indicator of power outages, but I didn't see anything. I didn't know that could have been an option. I guess I should have looked for that. I made many mistakes since this started, but unfortunately, I'm not done yet.

Mel claimed to be worried about me and wanted me to get on some medication. She had been pushing this for a while. She said other people see issues with me, but I didn't notice them. I have never been on any prescription drugs and fought this for a while, but ultimately, I thought it might help our situation and was worth a try. I made an appointment, but she demanded to go with me. I didn't think it was a big deal, but it obviously showed her control—especially when the doctor came in, and she would answer his questions to me or correct my answers. I was embarrassed but got through it. I ended up with pills for anxiety and depression. Mel was happy and got me one of those weekly pill organizers. I started taking them, but I felt no change. Both Mel and the doctor said it takes two or three months of taking them to see a difference. I was like, whatever. I had issues with one for depression, so I went back, and he changed it to something else. That fixed the side effect issue, but I never felt any different. I didn't get the hype. Pills rarely did anything for me. Maybe it's because I smoke weed.

During random arguments since maybe December, Mel had always proclaimed she would take a lie detector test to prove herself. So, I seriously started looking into them. The cost was around five hundred. I just needed to pick one out and set it up. I did some research and found one with good reviews. Looking back, I should have looked for one with the worst reviews (think about that for a minute). We needed a note from our therapist for some reason to have it done. That wasn't an issue, so I made an appointment with Walter and got a letter from him. Then I set it up for a Sunday, and we waited a couple of weeks.

The day for the lie detector came. It was a Sunday, about an hour and a half drive, so we left early. She dressed like she was going to a bar, and I asked why. She said we never go anywhere, and this is the first time going out in a while because of Covid. I didn't think much of it. Mel never acted nervous the whole way. I asked her if she was, and she said no. She put on a good innocent act and made fun of me for spending the money, but was also content with the idea so we could move forward. "Me too," I said. When we pulled into the parking lot, it was empty except for one other vehicle. We called, and he met us at the door and let us in. He was a thin guy in an ugly brown suit with a goofy, used car salesman look, probably in his forties – maybe early fifties. He had a small suite in the office building and had to keep the main doors locked. We followed him to his suite and went in. There was a small hallway with a wood bench and a couple of small rooms, and we went into one. It was a simple layout with his desk, test chair, and equipment. He said I couldn't be in the room because it may lead to false results. That caught me off guard, but my ignorance and overly-trusting self accepted it. Also, the way he ran the test was one subject, one question. I had to decide what was more important to me at the time. She was gaslighting me about the vibrator usage but sleeping with someone else was more important. He said we could come back in six months to take another one for the other subject. Direct questioning during the test was not the way he did things. Instead, Mel would write a statement down on paper, and during the test, she would be asked if she lied about what she wrote. The statement was supposed to be, "I did not have any sexual relations with anyone else besides (my name) in the last year." That was it. There would be five questions in total; the other four were known answer questions. The test would take a few hours for some reason and would take a break in between. I thought it was odd, but I had no experience with this, so I said ok. I gave Mel a quick peck and said, "Good luck," with a smirk. I fully anticipated a failed test and some much-needed mental relief. Then they walked me out and locked the door. I waited in the car because the seat was more comfortable than the wood bench, and I could listen to the radio and smoke if I wanted. After about an hour, he let Mel out, and she jumped in the car with me for a few minutes. I asked how it was going, and she said fine. She said she wasn't nervous or anything. She looked in the mirror, played with her hair, and reapplied lipstick. When it was time, he came back out to get her, and she went back in. About forty-five minutes later, they came back out. I got out of the car, and we talked for a minute. He said she passed and would send the results to my therapist in a few days. I was shocked and didn't know what to say. I probably thanked him. We got back in the car and were pulling out of the parking lot when she turned to me, smiling and excited, and said that it was easy and no problem if I wanted to take her back in six months for the vibrator issue. I was shocked because I knew she would fail that one. She touched me with one almost every night for months! She must have noticed my look of absolute shock and quickly said that on the second or third question, she answered yes and then no. Obviously, to give me some doubt about what really happened in there. She was too happy. My gut was telling me something was very wrong, again. Mal said, "You still don't believe me, do you?" I said, "No, no I don't," but she didn't care. She passed the lie detector, which is all that mattered to her. What I thought would finally end my nightmare only made things much worse. A few days later, Mel and I went to my therapist to get the results. Of course, Mel came too. I think she wanted to rub it in and get the therapists to help manipulate me even more. As Walter opened and read the results to us, he appeared to be in disbelief because of what I had been telling him. He had no choice but to agree and ask me to accept the results. I told them I would try. But everything in me was telling me something wasn't right. At the end of the session, Walter gave us the results, and I noticed it was just a typed-up letter. No graphs with question numbers, which is what I expected to see. I thought that wasn't right, but I had to let it go. If I didn't accept the results, I would look crazy. I briefly searched and found that some narcissists can beat a lie detector because they believe their lies. I had no choice but to believe Mel was so narcissistic that she passed somehow.

With only a week of vacation time left, which was reserved for hunting, I had to return to work. I looked sick, and the guys at work could tell. I gave them some excuses during my extended vacation, but I had to talk to them. It involved a co-worker, so I felt I had to tell the owner and my boss what was happening. I scheduled a private meeting at work the day after the lie detector, and I told them. All morning, my anxiety was through the roof. This is stuff you don't talk about. Maybe I should have just quit with no explanation. That's not who I am, though. No matter how uncomfortable the conversation, I thought I was doing the right thing. They were stunned about everything, and I could tell they had trouble believing me. Tim, one of the owners, is a friend of Mel's dad and went to Mel's first wedding about 20 years prior. You could say it was a small family company. I told them about the 3 a.m. driveway incident, and my boss was like, "Are you sure?" He continued and said, "I don't see Grump driving all that way in the middle of the night." It didn't sound right to me either, but that was what I knew. Only when I mentioned to my boss that I told him about some of the stuff months ago did he remember and start to believe me. I told them about the lie detector and that she passed somehow. My boss told me I'm not crazy; I'm not delusional, and Mel is mind fucking me. They told me they couldn't fire Grump, even if I had proof. I got their point, but I was hoping for a different reaction. Grump didn't have any issues working with me. I was the one with the problem, so I guess I'm the bad guy. Tim told me to use the front door to avoid Grump. I tried, and every day it was hard to go to work. The door between the shop and front office would often open throughout the day, and occasionally I would hear Grump's girly laugh or annoying voice over the other shop noises. I wore my headphones as much as possible. Then they started locking the front door, and I would have to knock. Sometimes someone would let me in, but I often had to sneak in the shop door. I asked Tim about it, and he said they must keep the door locked, so he gave me a key. After a couple of weeks, someone at work tested positive for Covid, so thankfully, I returned to working at home.

MARCH 2020 - JULY 2020

By March, we were still having a hard time, but I swore I'd never stop trying for us and our happiness. I would do my best to stay in a good mood and love her the way that she deserved. Mel was also struggling herself. She was depressed, and sometimes she just wanted to sleep all day and not be bothered.

"It's not that I don't love you," she told me. "I will never stop loving you. I need you to understand and not get an attitude with me every time I don't want to do something." Right now, her priority was on working out her depression. She needed my support more than anything. Sometimes, she just wanted to be held and hugged. I loved her so much it hurt sometimes. I just wanted to feel loved in return—maybe that was all I needed, too. A hug and to be held by a woman that I loved more than life.

She really was trying to work on her depression. On 3rd March, she announced that she was officially starting to work out. It was time for a change, she said, and she wanted me to join. Otherwise, she would have been fine doing it on her own. I was eager to join her, both in working out, and helping her deal with her depression.

On my birthday, Mel wished me a happy birthday, telling me that she hoped I had a good day and returned home quickly. Whatever I wanted to do today would be what we did. All I wanted was a good night with Mel. I loved her, and her body… After all these years, I still got butterflies when I was with her. No one turned me on like she did, and I just wanted to enjoy all of that without worrying or stressing. Work was busy, and it sucked, because it was one day that I didn't want to be busy. We never talked about what was bothering her, either. At least not properly… But I supposed that could wait for another day as we celebrated my birthday and enjoyed ourselves.

Relationships took a lot of work, but I knew we would never stop working for each other. I was certain that we would reach the ultimate relationship bliss at that time, even if it took us time and letting some guard down. Mel had feedback of her own—she wanted me to stop with my emotional attitude toward her.

"That's what was causing me to be depressed," she told me. She would think that everything was good, and then I would give her an attitude and she wouldn't know why. Mel wanted me to start communicating my feelings in a non-defensive manner so that we could work through them. She thought that I needed anxiety meds, too, and that I would benefit greatly from them.

"It's bad enough I hate work," she said. "I don't want to come home and be worried and sad there, too."

We both settled to take two weeks off from August 24 to 28, and then August 31 to September 4 to spend together. We were both in desperate need of a vacation, and we couldn't wait for those two blissful weeks to arrive.

Mel would occasionally tease me by wearing my favourite underwear the night before and leaving them for me to see. She knew it was something that drove me crazy. I would always send her a photograph and ask her not to throw them away.

"I won't throw them away," she always responded.

She had one dog, Rosey, and sometime mid-March, she told me that she wanted to have another one.

"Rosey needs a mate," she told me. It was an idea that she toyed with for months now. As long as the dog didn't tear up the house, and she took responsibility for them, which she already did a great job with, I had no issue with it. She was beyond excited about it— both about the possibility of a new dog and the two weeks we would get to spend together, away from work.

At one point, Mel realized that I had hacked into her email a while ago—Google told her, actually. It happened at a point in our lives when times had been tough. She was acting weird, which made me suspect she was cheating. I wasn't a creep, and I never wanted to be—I didn't look at her phone, nor did I ever want to. It usually only ended up in heartache and was unhealthy. The path to happiness was trust and never looking back into the past. I desperately wanted to move forward, and that unfortunately was a step forward. I was sure of it.

Mel's work announced the option of working at home may take a place soon (it later turned out that for the time being, they decided to only limit the number of outsiders allowed into the company). Mel was happy to work from home if she got to have double monitors. It was right before the first global lockdown when the world changed in a way, we never thought was even possible.

Around that time, she also struggled with soreness in her left hip that made it hard to walk. I thought we needed some exercise—our walks, and it probably wouldn't hurt to start stretching, too. Mel thought it may originate from sweeping the garage. I offered to massage her after work, telling her she should go to a massage place to get it sorted out properly. Despite all of her pain, which she managed with Excedrin and kratom, she wanted to wait for the coronavirus to settle down before going to the massage place. Neither of us knew it would be quite a wait. Until then, I decided to baby her.

Mel's sister was coming over later that day, too. They had come up with a cute name for the company they would open sometime in the future—Stitching sisters. I supported all of her dreams, including the one of a stitching business… And the adoption of a new puppy that she so desperately wanted.

No matter how hard the two of us tried, we always seemed to be caught in some kind of endless loop of issues we just couldn't snap out of. I couldn't help but feel like Mel didn't desire me anymore, and she'd accuse me of having an attitude with her.

"I love you and I have taken great strides to show you this. Just because I don't want to have sex at midnight doesn't mean I don't want you or desire or need you. It means I am tired and want to sleep. It's almost like you purposely set me up," she told me. Mel was also sick of the pit in her stomach that she constantly had, not knowing what type of attitude I would have with her, and she said she was sick of walking on eggshells constantly trying to make me happy, when nothing she did made me happy. She felt as if that was the one thing I focused on, which made her focus on it too—but in a negative light.

I wasn't mad, I was just still depressed and in somewhat of a funk I guess. I didn't feel as if I pushed her for anything, so I couldn't decipher where her attitude came from. One thing was for sure, however—I needed a break from things. I couldn't keep on going like that.

Mel felt like I didn't talk to her or communicate properly—in her opinion, I just skirted around stuff, and she couldn't know what was in my head.

"If you don't work with me, you'll always be working against me," she told me firmly. "If you don't want to fix things or make them better, then keep on doing what you're doing... But I'm not giving up."

Around the lockdown, Lizzy texted me asking whether she could stay with us if they locked everyone down. Before making a definite decision, I wanted to ask my better half first.

"I would never tell you no when it comes to your kids. Ever," Mel assured me, just as she assured me that she was doing her best to stop slacking in the intimacy department. She was getting her blood drawn to recheck her thyroid, vitamin D, and liver. She began taking supplements to help keep her body in check.

"I do want you. It's not that I don't. My body just doesn't want to cooperate with my brain sometimes," she said with a sigh as her test results returned. They all came back normal, except for one liver test that was low. As she tried her best, I did, too. I helped make her animal dreams come true by helping her purchase the bunnies that she had been raving for days about. They came at a price of $60 a piece, but that was a low price to pay for Mel's happiness.

By making our farm family a reality, she was more open to sex, too, giving me promises of intimacy and closeness that I so desperately craved with her.

I liked to continue moving forward with her in bed and wanted to try some of the things that I sketched up with her soon. I wanted to feel her.

It became somewhat transactional; I would try to do whatever I could to make her happy, hoping she'd want to enjoy me in return. I was open to trying different things that would make her want me. Mel said she just wanted me to be happy all the time—not just when we were intimate. She said it was what turned her on more than anything else—when I was positive. She was happy then, and in turn, wanted me.

When she felt like she slacked a little, she'd plan out date nights that became a regularity when she was depressed and couldn't give me what I needed.

"Just need to move forward, never back," she always said.

She tried her best to practice self-control and clean eating to feel better about her body, even if I told her many times over the course of years that I adored her body just as it was. Every curve, every crevice. Still, she was determined—starting off slowly this time so she wouldn't deprive herself of everything and slip further in the hole.

Unlike our relationship, our farm was flourishing. The newly purchased bunnies were doing fine, eating all of their hay. There were a lot of eggs and Mel and I took great care of our chickens. We've even had the barn cat come over to say hello. Then there was also another project that we started, which was re-building our deck. At least one thing was going just fine.

With the uncertainty of COVID, we weren't sure if we'd be able to do the vacation that we had planned… But the more we thought about it, we realized that we hadn't taken a vacation for the past two years. Mel wanted to go to Biltmore, get more wine, and see the gardens. We needed it—to reconnect and reenergize.

"I think I want to venture out and have you finger me tonight," she said in a text one morning. I thought we were finally getting closer to getting over the whole intimacy issue, but it never happened.

I spent my days working on the Mustang so that I could take a few things in and have them tig welded. I wanted to get as much done as possible because when the deck materials came, all of my focus would be on the deck. Mel, on the other hand, found one of the puppies that was available. He was only $850, she said, and she wanted to put in the deposit to hold him. She even suggested canceling the vacation—that we so desperately needed—so that we could get an extra $500.

I reluctantly agreed. How could I not, when she was so excited about it?

The name that she suggested for the puppy was Ollie, but she was quick to second-guess it because it sounded too close to Rosy, which she thought might confuse him. The breeder contacted her, telling her he'd have blue eyes, but they shouldn't be wonky since his parents weren't. That made her even more excited.

Still, there were issues we needed to handle, even with the new puppy and all. We were getting married in two months, and we still needed to figure out our intimacy issues and be one hundred percent full disclosure.

Mel said that there was something mentally wrong with me and that I was blaming all my problems on her when it is me that was the problem. She felt as if I didn't take accountability for my actions —like I was miserable and bringing her down constantly and she just couldn't let it happen. She said that I did it back in 2014, and that she wasn't going to let it happen again. She felt completely disconnected from me and it was killing her.

"You're tearing me apart at the seams, and I can't take it anymore, Matt," she told me.

I insisted that honesty would solve all our problems, but she told me that us not being together would solve them. She said that I had sucked the soul out of her—that she never lied to me about anything.

"When was the last time you took your medication?" she asked me as if they were a solution for our issues.

On 19th of July, Mel finally took the lie detector test.

Just a day later, she was diagnosed with psoriatic arthritis and acute inflammatory arthritis, both of which were auto-immune diseases. I, on the other hand, was given Prozac, buspirone, and a psychiatry referral. I had another therapy appointment in two weeks.

Mel insisted that through therapy and continuous work we could get through this together, yet one day she accidentally forwarded me a text that she sent to her sister.

Get this. He texts me, "On my way. I'll have dinner and then I'm going to my brother's to help me with those files." I freaking lost it. Started yelling told him he's out of his mind to think I'd cook for him so he could run off trying to prove I'm a liar! Get da fuck out!!! Oh, and he told me to stop brainwashing him...I'm sure something from his boss or weird ass belief he has.

We picked up Ollie, and he turned out to be horrible with crate training. Mel blamed the breeder for giving them too much freedom. Hopefully, after a week of crate training, he would get used to it and she could get some sleep since she was in charge of taking care of him. Mel covered the entire cage with blankets so he couldn't see anything. The issue was, Ollie didn't seem very much treat-motivated, so she figured she just needed to find the right treats.

SEVEN
DONE (AUGUST 2020 – MARCH 2021)

THINGS HAVE BEEN quiet but going nowhere. Mel and I talked, and she told me she wanted to see a therapist she picked herself. I thought maybe after she went by herself a few times, I could join, and hopefully, things would come out. I believed anything that happened ended at the beginning of March, and we would hold together. Mel picked out a therapist but seemed to struggle to go. I think she went two or three times. During that time, I was in the final stretch of getting my Mustang running, so I was often in the pole barn. After her last session, she came home, came out to the pole barn, and told me she had a few videos she wanted me to watch. She said they were about bipolar hypersexuality and that I have it and I needed to watch them. I did, and they described her almost perfectly. Depressed, on medication, side effects of the depression medication, always sleeping or pretending to be, many blankets, excessive self-pleasure, and multiple random partners. I didn't think too much about the multiple random partners because I didn't think it was an issue with her. I thought it was just Grump, but she passed a lie detector, right? I told Mel I watched the videos, and they described her actions. I tried talking calmly to her about it because if she was willing to share the videos and tell me about it, I thought maybe she was trying to reach out to me. During our talk, Mel again denied everything and said, "You think I'm still doing it?" She only let a few little things like that slip but nothing more. I tried for months, and I was defeated. I quit taking the useless medication Mel pushed me on. Nothing was working. Mel told me she was unable to make another appointment. Mel's therapist no longer wanted to see her after that last session. I will never know their conversations, but my guess is Mel freaked her out with the truth.

After Mel said, "You think I'm still doing it?" I thought that was suspicious, but maybe she was still doing something. I kept an eye on things, like her odometer or felt her car for heat in the mornings. I also checked the driveway for tracks and one day noticed some weeds had been freshly driven over at the end of the driveway where the larger stones were. Where the 3 a.m. car pulled in. The security cameras watched the entrances and could not reach the end of the driveway, so I grabbed a couple of trail cameras and set them up. I tried to conceal them, but it didn't work as I never got anything on them. I was always a step or two behind. Who knows? Mel may have seen them.

At this time, Mel and I started looking at phone providers. In a couple of months, we would lose the discounted plan with her brother-in-law, so we had to get our own. Mel offered to have Steve download and send me her phone records, so I thought, why not? Maybe Mel missed something; besides, after the account closes, the data would no longer be available. Steve was the account holder, so he had to do it. I was embarrassed to ask, basically telling them we were having problems. Plus, with Steve being Mel's brother-in-law, whom she has known since she was very young, I had no confidence in unaltered data. That and Mel offered, so I doubted anything was there. I looked into it, and I guess you can only go back a few months, and at that point, I thought I needed six months or more. I read there is a way to get older data, but it was a little hassle, and Steve wasn't going to do it. After a couple of weeks, Steve sent the past three months of data, but it showed nothing. With that over, finding a new provider with faster service at home was safe. Quick service was important because there were no other realistic options. We quickly found one five times faster than anything we had tried before. Now I was the account holder, and I could look at her usage and data, but by that time, I was tired of looking. And besides, she knew that I could see and never let anything slip.

Mel refused to talk, especially after the lie detector. So, I ended up sending a message to Grump's girl, Ann. She was curious to know what I knew, and once I told her, she claimed to have known that something was going on for two years, but she didn't know who the other person was. We exchanged some info, but neither of us had any proof. I told her she needed to not talk to him, get his phone, and run data recovery software on it. But instead, she went directly to him, and they argued. I guess they called Mel, had a conversation, and wanted me to join. Luckily Mel wasn't home at the time. I wanted nothing to do with it. I knew they would lie and make us look bad because we didn't have any proof. Ann told me afterward that they acted shadily, and she didn't believe either of them. She told me Grump refused to give her his phone, so she grabbed her stuff and left. I'm not sure what happened to them, nor do I care, but Grump missed the next few days from work. Mel was pissed and immediately unfriended me and all my friends and family on social media.

Work-wise, my bosses talked with Grump, and of course, he admitted nothing. But what I found odd was that they told me what Grump said. Grump told them he was shocked by the accusation, and when he drove home the day of the phone call, he just kept going and ended up in a different state and then turned around and drove the other way back into and across the state. Tim said Grump seemed distraught. He almost sounded empathetic towards him, but I think he knew it was bullshit, which is why he told me. Would an innocent man do that? I don't think so. After a few days, Ann said to me that Grump finally gave her his phone and admitted to sending memes, but not the ones I showed her. I don't think she ran any recovery software on it. I bet when Grump took his little drive, he was getting his phone wiped or maybe even a new phone. Oh well. Ann said she went back to him but didn't say anything else. Then we all blocked each other. Tim told me they couldn't legally fire Grump. I think he wanted to let me know he was using that as an excuse before I had a chance to ask. Again, I was the one with the problem. Oh well, I just went back to working at home. Later my boss told me that Grump said he doesn't blame me for anything. That's guilt for you. If someone legitimately almost ruined my nine-year relationship with false accusations of an affair, I would have different words. After Mel blocked me, she claimed social media didn't define us and still had hope for us. I had hope too, but that depended on Mel being honest.

The 2020 hunting season started, and normally we expected to have guests over. We didn't invite anyone because of our situation, but Gary and Bev still came over to hunt. Gary ended up shooting a young eight-point in the early season. I grabbed the tractor, and Mel came out to field dress it. Mel seemed to like the field dressing process more than hunting and would offer to gut any deer taken off the property. A little strange, but to each their own.

Mel and I were still hanging by a thread, but I think the last time we had sex was August or September. I don't remember; I don't keep a journal or keep track of that stuff. I was folding laundry one day and saw my favorite underwear of Mel's. I looked and found a couple of others with the same excessive wear and hole. I mentioned something to Mel and asked her to wear something sexy, maybe even pose for me. But it went the exact opposite of where I thought it would. Mel got angry and threw all her sexy underwear out. I didn't understand at all. Then she grabbed a few things and started sleeping in the upstairs spare bedroom every night. I tried one last guilt trip and bought her the fancy cordless vacuum she always wanted. Mel looked at it with tears in her eyes and mumbled, "Why?" I told her it was because I loved her and knew she always wanted one. But it didn't work; nothing worked. I tried everything—way beyond what a normal person would do. I didn't understand why Mel wouldn't even take the smallest step. Every time we talked, she would deny all and blame me. It seemed hopeless, but I kept praying for a miracle.

I had my hunting vacation coming up, but life was fucked up. Gary and Bev came out to hunt again. Gary shot a button buck, and Bev shot a doe. I think he knew things were bad and wanted to shoot some deer and get out. A couple of weeks later, Gary returned to pick up the rest of his hunting gear. So yeah, he knew. I hunted all day, every day, for eight straight days without seeing a shooter. On the ninth day, I had to work but made it out for the last hour and shot a good four and half-year-old buck. It was my best buck to date, but it was hard to smile because of what the rest of my life was going through. It was hard to enjoy anything in life. I told Mel, and she asked if I needed any help gutting. I told her no and did everything myself. We went to her dad's together on Thanksgiving, but things were quiet and awkward because I think everyone knew things were bad with us. I ended up going to my parents' for Thanksgiving dinner by myself. Then I headed to Chiefs hunting camp for a couple of days. I still had another tag, but I didn't use it. I did see a white coyote, but I missed it at only 30 yards. Maybe it was a sign. When I came home, I hit the half-bath from the garage entrance, and as I relieved myself, I looked at the sign Mel had hung above the toilet. I guess they call it wall art, and you can re-arrange letters to read anything. Mel put it together to say: "it's all shits and giggles until someone giggles and shits." I saw the word lies in there, so I re-arranged some letters. I made it read: "it's all shits and giggles until someone lies and shit." It stayed that way for a couple of months until she noticed. I felt I was entitled to the little jab, and I guess Mel did too because when she figured it out, she changed it back but didn't say one word to me.

Christmas came, but her family canceled because of covid. I still went to see my family, though. Between Mel and I, Christmas was canceled. It was the first year of not having a tree, stockings, or anything. It was sad. We decided on no exchange of gifts, but she got me a deer calendar, and I got her something cheap as well. I don't even remember what it was. We didn't even say Merry Christmas to each other. For New Year's Eve, I made her a card, and on the inside, I drew a stick figure of her in the center with two paths to take. The right path had honesty, forgiveness, and trust with a stick figure of me at the end. The left path had arguments, refinance, and moving with a stick figure of "not me" at the end. She still claimed to love me and never give up on us. But with no action, they were just hollow words. That night, we stayed home but didn't hang out with each other; no celebrating for us. I worked in the pole barn for a while, then stayed up until sometime after 3 a.m. to keep an eye on things.

In many of the arguments over the last year, Mel would say, "We'll have to sell the house," … which I hated, and she knew I hated. I told her I would never sell. We would have to get it refinanced in my name, and she would receive half of the equity to leave. Mel said she would not sign and didn't want to leave me. She claimed to have done nothing wrong and has never lied to me. I always wanted to believe her, but I knew it wasn't true. I had no proof, and she would rub that in my face whenever she had the chance. She told me I was delusional and obsessed with sex. That I think she masturbates all night and that I wanted her to be a sexual deviant. She said I was sick and needed professional help. She told her family that too. She never budged from her story.

I started talks with our mortgage guy back in October, but I put things off for some miracle. I prayed every day for it, but nothing changed. I contacted him again and told him I was ready. I had to have an appraisal done and file a ton of paperwork. Mel did nothing. She still didn't want to leave. Then, I noticed Mel went outside, walked through the snow to the corner of the front yard, turned around, and looked at the house. I followed the steps and thought, why was she taking a picture? Perhaps she was getting an appraisal on her own and just left it at that.

Since Mel was on my phone plan, I randomly looked at phone and text numbers but never saw anything. Now into February, I started to notice the data usage. She would run out of her allowed hot spot all the time and early in the month. She would need to use mine sometimes. I looked at her data usage and noticed a large amount of data consistently being used at 3 a.m., anywhere from 300Mb to over a gig. I asked her about it, but I asked her this way: "what do you do upstairs from 7 or 8 p.m. until 7 a.m.?" She said she reads books, watches TikTok, and browses online until midnight. Then I asked, "So you sleep from midnight to 7 a.m.?" She said, "Yes." So I said, "Well, it looks like the dog is using your phone at 3 a.m. because that's when a ton of data is being used." Mel got defensive, yelled at me for looking, and got on her own plan within days. I also checked energy usage, and there were spikes at 3 a.m. to match. I suspect FaceTime or a private webcam.

It was mid-February when Mel came into my room one night at 3:15 a.m. and woke me up frantically, telling me the neighbor's house was on fire. We rushed to the upstairs window to get a look. The police and ambulance were already there, and the fire truck showed up not long after. No one was hurt, but the home was destroyed. It was the same neighbor we had issues with. Although George worked on his farm daily, he didn't work anymore. I believed that he was taking advantage of the system. I think the fire was suspicious, especially after he made jealous comments about our new home. We watched for a few minutes, seemingly forcing us to communicate. Mel said the fire crackling woke her up, and she saw the reflections of flashing lights coming through the windows. I doubt she was sleeping but whatever. She acted distressed and asked for a hug. I thought about it and wanted to but said no and went back to sleep.

Now into March, more of the same limbo. My birthday came, and not a word was said between us. Weeks went by like this. We only talked when necessary. It was better than arguing. When the appraisal came back, Mel wanted a ridiculous amount of money. She still didn't want to leave for some reason. I had to talk to a real estate attorney. He told me what would happen, and it made sense. I went home and told Mel and then told her she could find an attorney and ask, but half of the equity would be the most she would get. According to the mortgage company, I could borrow almost that much. So, I made a deal with Mel to keep the ring to make up the difference, but she also wanted me to buy her a mattress for some reason. That and I had to give her time to find a new place. Because of the covid scare and the housing shortage, it wouldn't be easy. We ended up agreeing on two months.

End of March 2020, my closing day arrives. I head down to the title office in town and sign all the documents. It felt like signing divorce papers, and just like that, nothing legally tied us together anymore. A few days later, Mel went in and signed the quick claim deed and picked up her check. We were both still working at home, so it was tough. We didn't talk much, but I noticed she finally started to look for a new place.

August 2020 - March 2021

Mel was in therapy, too, but she still struggled. She wasn't sure our relationship was salvageable anymore.

"You have dissolved this relationship. You've beaten me into the ground, and I have done everything I possibly can to assure you that I love you. Nothing will be good enough for you," she said. "If you were willing to walk away from three children, what makes me believe you would stay and be happy with me?"

"How dare you say I walked away from my kids?" That was a low blow. "You know that's not true. She filed for divorce—not me. She wanted to get with a co-worker, thinking that things were greener on the other side."

She had very little fight left in her. She thought we were on the road to a happy forever life, but she thought she was mistaken. She tried to assure me that if she was to have cheated or masturbated every night as I had accused her of, she surely wouldn't have been putting forth the energy and time she has devoted to trying to work things out.

Mel said she'd rather be alone than with someone who considered her a cheater, a liar, secretive—someone who didn't trust her, who was always watching her, paranoid at every move she made. Someone who hated her music, movies, and tv shows. Someone who wasn't supportive—especially after coming from a seven-year addiction. That was how she saw me, sadly.

"If the only way you measure love is by having sex or being intimate in the bedroom, and not all the pieces that accompany me, then you don't love me nor do you know how to love. You are wasting away our years together with this, and it hurts me beyond belief," she said.

For the first time, I agreed with her. I just couldn't see this relationship working out if she wasn't honest with me, even if she tried desperately to get it back to normal by asking me to come with her to the Farmers and take Ollie for a ride. She went to shopping then, and I asked her to get me something for a broken heart—should be a bottle of truth and honesty, and it was something she could find down her heart aisle… But there was no mention of forgiveness in store for her just yet.

"Matt, I have told the truth and been nothing but honest with you," she told me. "I've done nothing wrong, so I'm not sure what you need to forgive."

She wanted to be happy, but she no longer thought we would be happy together. This has completely drained everything she had, she said. It put us both into an uncomfortable situation where there were choices to be faced. Either we could do a home equity loan and she would leave, or we could sell the house.

"I can't do this anymore. I am a good person and I have never lied to you. I went through a rough patch coming off drugs and you weren't there to support me. At all," she said to me. I didn't even understand where she found the audacity to say those words after everything I had done for her. She thought that instead, I made accusations upon accusations which had proven to be false.

Mel accused me of not being willing to do any self-reflection or get the help necessary to repair this relationship, after all that I had tried to do—it still wasn't good enough for her.

I was trying, but it wasn't good enough for her.

"I'll call and make an appointment for myself with the therapist tomorrow. I've been doing everything you've asked of me," I told her. Mel shook her head at those words.

"No. You haven't tried everything. When will you stop blaming me for everything and take responsibility for your part in all of this? I told you I wanted to see the therapist with you, and you somehow are still trying to manage to go by yourself, without me," she said. She felt like I could run away all day long and stay in the pole barn for hours to get away, rather than manning up and having a decent conversation with her.

Mel was also annoyed because she felt like she had to ask me to take medicine every day.

"Do you remember the promise you made my dad? How would you do everything to make me happy and you'll love me and be kind and give me safety for the rest of my life?" she asked me in an attempt to turn this around, before accusing me of covering things up with pot or yelling and running away into my pole barn.

After one of her therapies, she sent me several videos from a YouTube series about bipolar hypersexuality. She said I had it and should watch them, which I did. It described her perfectly, except for the multiple random partners—or so I thought at the time.

I refused to stop fighting for us. I told her I would make an appointment with my therapist. I loved her with all my being and couldn't imagine life without her. I was strong enough to admit that I was in a really bad place, and I needed to get out of it. It felt like the bad place was ending, but I needed help, and I needed her and her love to get me through this. I also promised to consistently take my medicine to try and get better.

Mel said she had always been there.

"I haven't wavered one bit because I know this is something with your brain that even you can't control," she said, assuring me that there hadn't been anyone else. She thought stopping the pot and making an appointment with my therapist was a good step forward.

"A psychiatrist may also be beneficial," she said. "I'm not

gaslighting you, either. I'm being supportive the best way I know how, but I also deserve happiness. We don't have much life left to live, and I don't want to live it miserable and alone. I need you. You are my life partner."

We just had to get my brain better, she assured me, pointing out that she could easily run, but she had chosen to stay.

The next day, Mel went to therapy. Her therapist was late; she waited for her as she couldn't see her car, telling me that she'd give it another ten minutes before she called it and left.

"You take a nap too? I'm really busy here. No word from Steve?" I texted her.

Her response was instant and it read, "Why don't you be mean and rude to Liz or Jenna or your ex, or your bosses? Quit abusing me. I've sent Steve a text."

I found her response hilarious. "No abuse, just asking. No need to get a defensive life partner. The family still loves you," I texted her back.

"I'm not defensive. I'm sick of it, and I'm not taking it anymore. Every time you do that, you just push me further away," she responded. "Ask Steve yourself and leave me out of it. Next thing you know, you'll be accusing me or Steve of altering records."

"Not at all. It is what it is. I'm not pushing at all. I just asked a question, that is all. I will not ask again. Geez..." I told her.

Part of my healing process included unfriending and blocking Grump and Kurt on social media. I didn't believe Steve couldn't retrieve texts—while I knew content couldn't be retrieved, but numbers and times could be. Still, I had to drop it, because I wasn't pushing anymore, and I needed to move forward.

"Steve wouldn't lie to you, Matt," she assured me. "Did you know you sent a blank email to Steve and me at midnight last night?"

"No, must've been a fat finger..." I responded. Mel laughed at my words.

"Nothing on you," she told me lovingly.

"Ego?" I questioned her words. It had been mentioned once or twice before.

"Not even that. I'm not letting that bring us down. Steve is family, and has been for 27 years, so of course, I'll protect him."

Mel was able to sense the fact I wasn't happy by the lack of good morning messages. She was tired of the back and forth with me, claiming that smoking pot had a lot to do with it. She couldn't handle this up and down all the time.

"I don't deserve to live like this. If you can't make the changes necessary to move forward, then separating is our only option," she warned me. It wasn't what she wanted, but she refused to continue living the way we are living. "Make me and your family your priority, and everything will fall into place."

She refused to spend hundreds of dollars on therapy when I wouldn't even talk—which was ridiculous, considering the lack of honesty on her end.

We would try to take it slow and enjoy each other—break the monotony between us with our date nights that used to help, but right now, nothing seemed to help.

Mel accused me of having a new, private email account that she should not have found out about. I told her it wasn't secret or private, reminding her that she had a secret account of her own.

She claimed to have told me about her creeper account a long time ago—I just didn't remember because I didn't listen to a word she said. She accused me that I only cared about myself.

I just wanted the truth.

"Question for you...have you ever met Marlene's husband? You know, the one with heroin issues?" I asked her.

"No, I have never met Marlene's husband. Why do you ask?"

I was calm with my response. "Just wondering if you were getting drugs from him. Not accusing, just asking a question."

"I get Norco from the pharmacy. The only other person I got pills from was daddy Dave, and you were there. I never have used heroin. I don't know why you have these thoughts and continue to have them but it's extremely counterproductive," she responded. It felt like there would never be a normal life with us again. If you asked Mel, it was because of everything I had put her through and continued to put her through. I, on the other hand, suspected it was because of her dishonesty.

She felt like every day it was something new—some new thought and accusation.

"I don't want to live my life like this at all. I want a partner who shares life with me and supports me. I don't need someone who is always against me, doesn't trust me, or feels the need to control my every move."

She felt like she dedicated the last four years of her life to me and our life—to building our dreams. She claimed that just because she didn't have sex with me or was intimate every day of the week, I created issues, when what I really should be doing was finding the good in us and working to better our future.

"So long as you continue to smoke weed, I'm fairly confident you will not be able to move forward as it alters your perception and your ability to think clearly," she said. Mel thought that she dealt with enough of this and would no longer partake in my negative attitude. "Unless you want to move forward and improve the way you live life, aka quit smoking weed, then I don't want to be a part of your life."

Mel continued to accuse me of smoking too much weed, even going as far as to say that I did it behind her back. She accused me of being a liar and not telling her things—telling me that I was the one that made things up and kept stuff away from her. She said she was trying to be supportive of me quitting, instead of being shitty and accusing me of terrible things, but it rarely felt like that.

I tried therapy, but it didn't change the past. I tried pills, it didn't change the past. I would try to stop smoking weed for a while and see what it did—but I was guessing it wasn't going to change the past, either.

"And anyone with any sense at all would have left months ago. I had hope for us, but not anymore," Mel told me during one of the arguments. "I'm pulling the supply cord to my feelings for you."

She claimed that none of her actions were to control me; that they came from a place of care and concern for my own well-being, but if she really meant that… Honesty would have gone a long way.

I had been through hell, and I was just trying to keep my head up and stay positive. I was just trying to keep pushing and not give up. I loved her; I lusted after her… But those feelings weren't reciprocated. I waited and waited, and nothing ever changed.

Mel clearly showed that she wasn't happy with me. She said that she deserved to be happy, but she was no longer getting that with me.

"I'm not letting you steal one more minute of my self-worth and happiness. You've taken enough from me," she said. "You can put me through a thousand lie detector tests and every single one of them would come back not deceptive. Yours on the other hand…" She shook her head. She claimed that my anger came from fear and frustration.

"If you only got out of your own way, you could be one hell of a man. Ask yourself one question… If you were to die today, what would people say about you?" I didn't know, nor did it matter. What mattered was the two of us—at least in my eyes.

Mel said that my brother told her ages ago that I was an asshole, and she should have listened to her brain rather than her heart. It sounded as if she thought she was better off without me than she was with me—as if she was regretting walking back into my life.

I was just a nice guy that got walked all over. All the time. My main problem was that I never said no, aside from occasionally going to the grocery stores.

"If I asked anyone who knows you, 'nice guy' would not come to their mind," she assured me.

Mel thought that I did nothing in our relationship aside from things that involved money. According to her, I never came up to her and rubbed her shoulders without her asking. I never did dishes or the laundry just because I wanted to be nice. I never went shopping and picked her something up out of the goodness of my heart. I never said, "Hop in the car, let's go for a joyride." I never said, "Why don't you go out and I'll watch the dogs?" I never did something for one of her family members out of the kindness of my heart. I never said, "I'm sorry you had a bad day, would you like to go out to grab something to eat?" I never went somewhere she wanted to go because I wanted her to be happy even if it meant that I was uncomfortable.

It was all about the things that she thought I *didn't* do, and she forgot about everything that I did do.

She'd often bring up pictures that were sitting on the floor that needed to be hung up in my office—we had lived there for two years, she said, and if it weren't for her, all the pictures would still be on the floor. Collecting dust. Apparently, the way she saw it, I didn't care about anything unless it had to do with my dick.

The truth is, I rubbed her back a few times without her asking. I constantly got her Dr. Pepper without her asking. I helped with the flower beds, hog shack clean-ups and I went for walks with her whenever she asked me. I always watched her shows with her. A lot of the things that she was saying weren't true.

I tried to be as accommodating and as nice as possible. We

haven't had sex for three weeks. I haven't tried talking her into it...
And I only touched myself once in those three weeks. As hard as
it was.

It seemed like she was just trying to justify herself leaving me,
and making it my fault. All she cared about was trying to look good
in front of her family, and make me look bad.

"Your words mean zero to me. I bet your kids would agree. Hell,
your dad would agree. How much have you paid him back? Does
he know the couple thousand dollars you've sunk into your car?
Priorities. Something you don't know a whole lot about, eh?" she
said. She thought she wasn't bad—it was just me that refused to
take accountability for my actions. "I don't need to make you look
bad; you do that on your own."

I was so bad that I went to therapy. I was so bad I got on
prescription drugs. She continuously gaslit me, taking no responsibility for her action. Gaslighting.

All that time, all I wanted was to love her and give her everything I was and everything I had. I just wanted to be on top of the
world with her. All I needed was some honesty so that I could
forgive and move forward. I was begging her to save us.

Mel said that it was our life, our house we were turning into our
home, our dreams. I was her man, and she was my woman. She
didn't know how we got so derailed, but we were in this life
together.

"Without a doubt and with all my soul, I have not seen,
touched, or been with anyone but you. There is no one I think of
or want to be with but you," she told me, adding that she had no
understanding of what has happened. If she did, by now she
would have said something because she was as miserable as
I was.

If we were wanting to move forward, we had to stop with this
nonsense. Stop hurting each other, stop the negativity, stop pointing

fingers, and we needed to start living in the moment, start supporting each other, and start falling in love once again.

She swore that from this day on, she would no longer be mean or put me down. She swore that she would not nag or say and do hurtful things out of spite. She swore to support me and do things I liked and wanted to do. She swore not to react to negativity or meanness. She was willing to work toward making this relationship fulfilling.

"I am here. I always have been and always will be no matter how ugly things get," she told me, and for a moment there, I believed her.

I agreed. I was miserable without her love. We had to do something about the current situation and our frame of mind. We had to try something different because what we were doing currently wasn't working for us or our happiness. I had issues with what I felt were unanswered questions and also her wanting and desire toward me. That was all. If those things could be resolved, I knew I would be good.

Mel wanted me to stop smoking pot. Maybe not quit altogether right away, but at least have my last hit on my way home from work, and much less on the weekends. She knew how hard it was.

She wanted our communication to improve too.

She was no longer friends with me or any of my family, and I was no longer friends with Carrie. Mel said it took me a week before I realized it—she didn't want anyone else involved in our life, and that was the only way she knew how. She thought I overanalyzed Facebook—and once we finally managed to move forward, she hoped that was going to change. Grinch and his girlfriend had unfriended her too. While she couldn't isolate herself from the world, she also didn't want anyone else involved between us.

She even blocked me in all of her fury a few days ago, and it took her a few days to undo that.

Aside from the difficulties in our relationship, my work on Mustang also wasn't going well. I was starting to lose all hope, and Mel tried to convince me to think more positively—to change my mindset.

She told me that she lost her mom in 2016, went through hell and back with building the house, lost her cat of fourteen years, got shingles and skin cancer, went through horrible withdrawals from a seven-year addiction to pain medicine, and was going through a battle with her life partner who was convinced that she was cheating on him. It was hard to stay positive for her too, but she said it was a choice she made daily.

I offered to get her flowers and a new vacuum if only she came clean. Everyone would finally be able to enjoy life again—everything would finally go back to the way it used to be. Mel claimed that there was nothing for her to come clean with.

She was upset that I had time for things that I wanted, but when it came to texting something as simple as 'I love you,' I just couldn't do it. It would make her feel like she bothered me or inconvenienced me. She claimed to be stressed out too, but she still made time out of her day for me, out of love and care, not out of obligation.

I didn't feel like she loved me, and it felt awkward. She said she did, but her actions spoke louder than her words. And it had been like this for years now. I needed her to talk to me about things, and she never did. She just kept things bottled up, and I saw it through actions and reactions and the look of guilt. I wasn't sure when it would pass, so I waited and prayed. I didn't want to argue—I was trying to be happy and live my life. If she wanted to be a part of it, she'd have to start talking to me.

She once asked me what I wanted for the sweetest day, and I said a running Mustang. Right now, it was to be happy and move forward with my life. I was waiting for the one thing that would bring me there, but I would not be able to wait much longer.

Mel kept saying that she has spent the last year telling me and proving to me that she didn't cheat or have an affair. She said she was done with all of this, yet she kept saying that she was not leaving the dream that she has been building.

I didn't understand why she was torturing me like this. It was clear that she didn't want me or desire me in any way. This whole thing told me there was no way she loved me. Why would she stay with someone she didn't love or desire? She would no longer touch me, and now I wouldn't touch her. I knew she was happy with that and could lay in bed buzzing all night, not needing me for anything but pay the bills.

Again, she retorted by saying that she didn't do anything for the millionth time. She claimed that it was my insecurities that made me lose everything. I lost my first marriage and kids because of it apparently, and now I was pushing her out of her life too. She thought I'd rather blame everyone for issues of my own.

"You've done it your entire life," she told me. "You're so angry at everything and everyone, especially when you don't get your own way."

Mel claimed to have taken all the accusations and the lie detector tests, cried countless tears over this, and withstood being alone every single evening while I was working on the Mustang... She said she put on a happy face in front of my co-workers and family, and I just kept pushing her further and further away and calling me a liar, a cheater, and a narcissistic pathological liar.

"I am none of those things," she claimed. "I am a wonderful, good-hearted, loving person and how I am treated is a direct reflection of how I treat others."

She thought I was the only person that couldn't see it—stating that perhaps twenty-plus years of doing drugs had me blinded...

Saying that maybe I never learned how to self-reflect. It wasn't her that was causing me to be tortured—it was my own self.

I couldn't stand her gaslighting. I had enough. There were a lot of things left unanswered. What was on the audio? What was in the black bag with the white floral pattern? Where did the blood come from on the vibrating shaver? What did she go upstairs for on New Year's Eve? Who pulled into the driveway at 3 a.m., and why did she open the garage door that same night after I went to sleep? What did she use to touch me with while spooning? What was the antenna thing with balls on the ends down when I put my hand down there? Why did she tighten her legs so hard when she told me to check? There was more, but there was no point in bringing it up. Clearly, she would take it all to her grave, and this wasn't going anywhere. I wasn't sure why she was hiding so much from me. Well, actually I did know why, but she refused to come clean about anything. What was clear, was that she didn't love me. She loved torture.

Mel stuck by her words. She said she never cheated on me or had any type of relationship with anyone but me for the past five years, nor had she masturbated or used vibrators or any other devices every night while lying next to me.

"At this point, you need to make a choice, Matt. Either we move forward and live life together as partners, or we sell the house and go our separate ways. There are no other options at this point," Mel told me. She seemed like she didn't want the latter, and she wanted to continue the life and dream we were building, but if I couldn't get it unstuck in my mind, then we wouldn't be able to go on like this.

She didn't want to fight or bicker, she said. She just wanted us to be happy. And it was up to me to make the choice—she loved me, and always would.

I wasn't stupid—all of it was up to her, actually. It was pretty clear at this point that I wanted to make things work too, but she had to start from the beginning. She had to be honest and tell me everything.

There was no other option for us to make things work and I knew it. It was up to her. Why did she hide sexual stuff from me? Why did she throw stuff away, when all I wanted was to share, explore and move forward with her? She was doing the opposite of what a life partner would do. She was hiding things from me, and refusing to admit to anything.

I wasn't stupid, I had a big heart, and she knew it.

The only other thing I could think of was that she loved torture and she had an alternate personality at night when it comes to sexual stuff. Why would she stay with me if she never wanted me in that way, unless it was a torture thing?

I wasn't going to sell the house as she suggested, so I'd have to work on paying off all my debt, and hopefully, I'd be able to qualify to refinance on my own and get an equity loan for her. It was either that, or she signed a quick claim deed, giving up her rights to the house. So, until then, I guessed we'd continue to struggle.

My boss asked me to go into the shop and talk to Paul about something. I went to grab my safety glasses, and he remembered my situation and said he'd go get Paul and ask him to come up to our cubes to discuss. It worked out this time, but one of these days it wouldn't. I kept praying this nightmare would end—I just wanted Mel to stop torturing me, tell me the truth and confirm what I already knew so that I knew whom I needed to avoid for the rest of my life and could finally move forward mentally.

Mel tried to gaslight me once more, telling me that I was poisoning myself with my beliefs, thoughts, and assumptions. That was why she suggested antidepressants and anxiety medication—to help balance me out a little bit. She was adamant that there was nothing wrong with taking them.

I supposed that the only choice we had was to continue being roommates until we could get our financials straight. I wanted her to limit talking to me unless absolutely necessary only, and I was not going to be attending Thanksgiving or Christmas with her family either.

My days became torture, plagued by thoughts of what Mel was doing behind my back. What hurt me the most was the fact that she claimed she always did the right thing, as she had for a good ten years now. She said she didn't have to prove herself to anyone, including me. She said that she hadn't done a thing to hurt anyone, least of all me, but I knew she was lying.

She didn't love me, but I couldn't figure out why she would stay. It was obvious that there was another man that she wanted. Perhaps he left her, or better yet, refused to leave their old lady for her. There was no way we could have a good relationship with her fantasizing about him while lying next to me.

What was wrong with her?

I begged her for a name. That was all that I needed.

Mel admitted that she sent memes back and forth with Grump, but it was something she said she told me about—something purely out of fun. She said she texted Jake about hunting stuff. She talked to some guys at work about hunting and our house. But she firmly stated that she had no feelings or desires for anyone other than me. She wasn't a sex thing that I desperately wanted, nor did she want to be touched and have sex all the time, but that didn't mean there was someone else.

She asked me to love her for who she was, not what I wished her to be.

Mel thought that I was a weak-minded narcissist that berated her, controlled her, fucked with her head, punished her, and when I didn't get what I wanted… Ignored her, isolated her, walked away and closed down.

"Reread that narcissist meme you sent me, Matt, because it's exactly what you're doing," she said. All of a sudden it was me that lured her in with my bullshit lies and words, it was me that took advantage of her when she was in a low spot. It was me that put a rope around her financially.

She claimed that everything I said to her was a projection of my inner self. I supposedly conjured all these assumptions and stuck to a narrative so concrete in my brain, that I had even gone as far as rallying others to believe my story. She made me out to seem like some lunatic that called her names, video-taped her every move, checked her phone and social media, downloaded her data, monitored her through GPS...

Mel used me, plain and simple, and now she was afraid to tell me the truth. I didn't want to spend the rest of my life with a liar, and I was done being her foreplay bitch, only for her to get her main play after I fell asleep. I no longer cared who or what she fucked—she could do whatever the hell she wanted.

I was done.

She could take the shirts back to Kohl's and put the money toward the treadmill. She could also save the dog wire for her next place. I wanted to get it rolling so she could be with her 3 a.m. dick.

Mel refused to leave, saying it was her house too, and that she would put in the dog fence this weekend.

The funny thing was, I would have been a lot more accepting than she thought. I wasn't looking for revenge or anything bad. I just wanted my mind right, so we could move forward.

Mel tried to reason with me. She said she knew and understood why I thought there was someone else—because she always said no to sex. But it had nothing to do with someone else or not loving me, or the "3 a.m. dick." It all had to do with several things. First was how I made her feel and our emotional connections. The second was how she felt about herself. The third was that when she did have sex, she'd experience pain, which she found embarrassing to talk about. She said that when I slid inside of her, it felt like her bladder was being jabbed and she felt like she had to go to the bathroom. Other times, she'd get UTIs which were uncomfortable. She could never orgasm just from vaginal sex—she had had a few when we used the vibrator a long time ago, and that was the most embarrassing of anything she could tell a person.

She said she knew I wouldn't believe her because sex was so wonderful to me so I thought she must have been getting it from someone else, and that was just not the case. She wanted nothing more than to be close to me again... Even closer for that matter. She said she wanted me to hold her, and she wanted to make love to me again.

She said she accepted and wholeheartedly took the blame for saying no all the time, and what that had done to me, yet she refused to tell me the truth.

Our bickering continued to go back and forth. I simply couldn't accept the lack of honesty. I deserved better than that. I had given her all she ever wanted—all she ever needed, and she couldn't even be honest with me.

Questions reeled inside my head. Did I truly mean that little to her? Did I really not deserve honesty? Did I truly not deserve answers to questions that haunted me after all these years we had spent together?

Right now, we were nothing but roommates forced to live together. Seeing her every day hurt and was a constant reminder of everything that she continued to put me through. A part of me began to hate her for it.

We spent Thanksgiving separately. I left to spend it with my kids, as there was no way I was going to spend the holiday with someone as deceitful as her.

"Tell everyone I said hi and happy Thanksgiving," she texted me. "And see if you can bring me back a pink T-shirt or hoodie from up north somewhere, please."

I scoffed at the text. I couldn't believe the audacity that she had to ask for something after not having the basic human decency to be honest with me.

"See if you can muster up the nerve to tell me," I responded. Her answer was almost instant.

"So, let go of me, Matt. Why don't you just say you want to be alone?" It was almost as if she wanted me to leave. She wanted to be left, so she could expand her lies and tell everyone that it was me that was the bad guy. It would be just another lie on a pile that she shared with me every day. "If I'm such a piece of shit to you, then go find better. But you pushing me away from you isn't working. I simply asked for a t-shirt or hoodie. I'll pay for it. I'm not looking for you to go out of your way and do something nice because I know that's not who you are."

It was funny how now that I called her out on her bullshit she was saying such things. All these years we spent together, along with all the money I spent on her, she had no such complaints. No, they rose now that she could no longer deceive me.

I didn't respond. An hour later, she texted me once again to make sure that she got her point across.

"I'm blocking you because I don't want another cry myself to sleep again. Matt, I'm done being your fucking muse. Unless you have pictures of me in bed with a guy, or you can physically show me a text or a voicemail some guy left on my phone, then it's all made-up bullshit that is stemming from your own insecurities. This is a very shitty way to break up an eight-and-a-half-year relation-ship. Seeing how you've been trying for a year, and *still* have zero evidence or proof, then all I can say is thanks for ruining a great fucking life together," her text said. I remained firm in my stance.

"It's pretty simple. Be completely honest with me, and things go back to normal. If not, then things won't ever be the same again. I promise you that."

Upon my return from the Thanksgiving celebration, the tension continued. Mel would complain about the tiniest things, like doing the laundry late. I'd often remind her of things that needed to be bought for the household. Picking up some honesty and doing the right thing included.

EIGHT
THE LIST (APRIL 2021)

It was late April, and for some reason, I thought about the bi-polar hypersexuality thing Mel accused me of almost a year ago. I decided to look into it again. Everything was the same, and towards the end, I heard those three words again, multiple random partners, but this time something clicked. Although I had no proof, I knew Mel was lying about the toys and that she had an affair, but I never thought of multiple random partners as a possibility. Her complete lack of admitting anything always had me thinking there was more, a lot more. Something so bad that she would throw away everything we built together so she didn't have to tell me. An image I saw a year prior popped into my mind. I looked on the computer, found the image, and examined it more closely this time. It was a list of names. My name was on it too. I remembered looking at it before but couldn't make sense of it at the time. I just filed it away. It turns out it would be the most incriminating circumstantial evidence I had, and it made me sick. It looked like this:

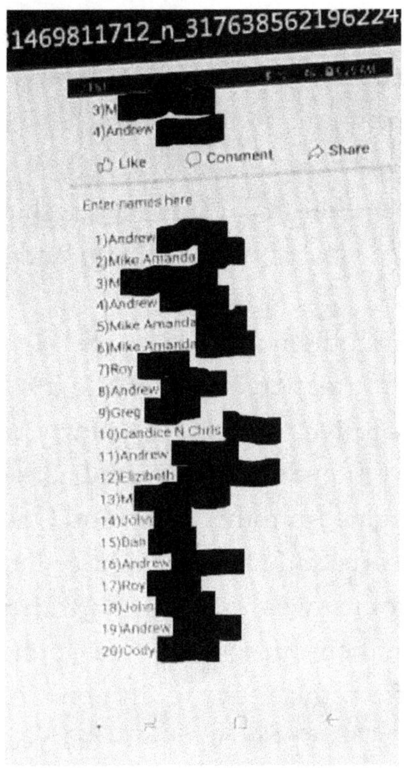

The image came from her phone but what was strange was the upper left corner displayed a different carrier than who we used. I quickly figured out that she must have taken a picture from her phone of another phone displaying the list of names. Mel had another phone. That explains her willingness to have me check her phone and get the data from Steve. Then I remembered one of the audio recordings where I heard what I thought was Mel opening a package in the middle of the night. What I thought was a new toy at the time must have been the secret phone. I remember seeing a couple of images from her phone scan from an AT&T website, but it was nothing incriminating. I assumed it was random auto-saved images, but I made a mental note of them. Now I know. I'm not controlling or jealous, so I never checked her bank or credit cards. If I did, I probably would have found her phone expenses, unexplained cash withdrawals, or possibly hotel stays. I'm not sure why she took that picture. Maybe because I was getting close, she decided to dump the secret phone, but the list has a "like, comment, share" on it as if it were created on Facebook. It was probably somewhere in her fake profile that I missed, or she deleted it before I discovered it. Either way, she slipped up, and I found the largest piece of the puzzle.

I began to research the names on the list. I found some pictures and a little public information on them. The first thing I noticed was even though they all lived within, say, thirty miles, none of them were even friends of friends on social media. Some of their pictures were also on her phone from the year prior. One was a guy and his mom with some hearts added in. He sort of looked like a younger version of me. Another was a family portrait picture of a couple who looked to be in their thirties and their young children. The ages on the list ranged from thirty-one to fifty-one. At the time, Mel was forty-one, so it looks like plus or minus ten years was her requirement. There were two couples on the list. One was the family couple already mentioned (listed once), and the other was listed three times. The couple on there three times, the guy is a registered sex offender, and the girl had discreet NSA hook-ups embedded in her Pinterest page. The only picture I found of her was half of her face. She remained hidden, and probably for a good reason. I call them the dirty couple. One of the guys on the list appeared tall with a mongoloid looking face. The last person on the list was a bodybuilder guy. There was no shortage of pictures of him on the internet. I have no idea how many of the singles were married and cheating, nor do I care. It wouldn't surprise me, though. Their morals were low enough to sneak into my house and do what they did while I was sleeping. I didn't attempt to contact anyone on the list, nor will I. They wouldn't admit to anything; even if they did, it wouldn't change anything. I later learned the single female was married and happened to be a sister to the wife in the family couple. Mel must have had a good referral.

Everything that happened started to make sense. I remembered Mel asking me back in late January or early February for me to be bigger and what would happen if I needed to protect her. I thought it was odd to say, so it stuck with me. That must have been after she was with the bodybuilder. Then the three a.m. driveway incident made sense. Although they had a long-term affair, it wasn't Grump; he was too lazy like everyone else agreed. It was someone on the list. And the audio files were not Mel leaving the bedroom at night to watch porn. She was leaving the bedroom to practice porn. When I heard the dog barking and growling on multiple occasions, then Mel telling the dog to be quiet, and it was just deer. It was actually people. It was shocking, and I didn't want to believe what I was thinking, but I knew that was the truth. Mel was quiet and must have instructed them to be silent as well. No talking, phones, belts, zippers, keys, nothing that made noise. Everything made sense. I felt sick and helpless. How much more was there?

I decided to approach Mel and ask about the list. We were already destroyed with no chance of making up, but I went upstairs and asked her about it anyway. She was lying on the bed reading an addiction book. I asked her where the list came from, and I showed it to her. She looked concerned and worried at first, but blew it off, said she didn't know and asked where I got it. I told her it was from her phone. She claimed not to know where it came from and acted like it wasn't a big deal. I knew and could see it in her eyes. I didn't want to get into it, so I left her alone and went back downstairs. The next morning, before I even got out of bed, Mel rushed downstairs, knocked on my door, and said she knew where the list came from. She was anxious to tell me and said it must have been people who looked at her LinkedIn page. Then I asked, "So you wrote those names down, including mine?" She said, "Yes." So I calmly replied,

"You just admitted to having a secret phone because that was from a different carrier. Plus, why write down the same name multiple times? Why my name? Plus, no one has a couple's LinkedIn accounts." She had no answers and started to blame me. She said I imagined things, always thinking about sex, that I wanted her to be a sexual deviant, and that I was sick and needed professional help. As Mel retreated upstairs, I yelled back that it was *her* that needed professional help. Going back and forth wasn't going to help or change anything, so I didn't pursue it. After that point, our arguments turned into short, screaming matches. I called her a whore many times and asked if she got paid. I don't think she did because it wasn't about money for her. But she never admitted anything, so I don't know. I felt terrible saying those things, but I did anyway. At the time, I couldn't control myself. I had no other words.

Then I figured out the timeline. At first, I thought it was a two-month period, but going by how many times we were together, it was only a month. A list of twenty in a month. I knew she was going full bore all of February, so double that number. I'm sure there were many more before and after this manic episode.

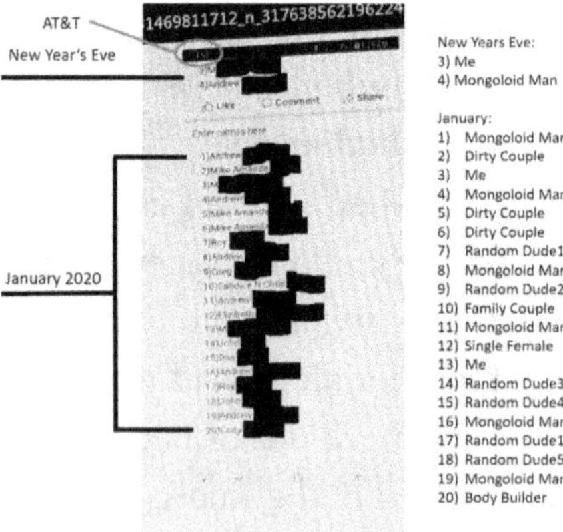

The beginning of the list shows the last two people for the month prior. I believe that was the month she started with strangers. It was

December 2019. At the top of the list was me being the third and the fourth being Mongoloid Man. That was New Year's Eve, and now I know why Mel ran upstairs. It might have been to put something sexy on like she admitted months later, but it wasn't for me. I regretted not recording audio that night, but at this point, it wouldn't have mattered anyway. I would guess the first was Mongoloid Man, and the second was the Grump. Now that I think about it, Mel went to stay with her sister after my work's Christmas dinner party. According to the memes that I believe were shared that night, I think she tried to break it off with Grump to start on her high-risk stranger adventures. But she ended up staying at her sister's that weekend and more, so I think the Grump affair continued.

Next, I wondered about the audio file where I heard her masturbating. Did she have someone sneak into our room while I slept right next to her? I listened to it many times and didn't hear anyone else. I think she wanted to ensure she could still do her trick before performing it on me. There were other instances during that period that was odd that I remember. She always hated morning sex and never gave me any. During that period, she offered once, and it felt like she was worn out. I assumed it was because of her many hours of nightly self-pleasure, but now I know. I also remember a morning pretzel session where Mel asked me to rub her head, which was not unusual, but this time I felt something wet in her hair. At the time, I thought it was maybe lotion for her dermatitis and didn't say anything and just avoided that spot. But now that I think about it, I put that stuff on her head before, and it was like a foam that quickly dissipated. That didn't feel the same and is another example of her sadistic torture.

There were other little things as well. After pretzel sessions, Mel sometimes yelled at me to hurry up my nightcap, rushing me back to bed. Always asking me what time I would be home from work. I can remember a time or two when I got into bed, and there was already a wet spot on the bed. I even mentioned it, and she just said she napped earlier and was sweating. At the time, that was believable because of her seemingly non-stop self-pleasure. I also remember lying in bed a couple of nights and hearing sounds like someone taking a few steps on the roof or upstairs. Since it was the first winter in the new home, I assumed it was the foundation settling, but maybe not. A few mornings, I woke up to find the garage door unlocked, both entry to the house and outside.

One morning, I walked out to the garage, and I could have sworn Mel's car was warm. That might have been after the family couple night. Maybe the family couple wouldn't leave their kids in the middle of the night, so perhaps Mel went to their place. I suppose it could have been the single female as well. I don't think a single female would sneak into an unknown house at night, but you never know. The single female lived in another state, but her sister was local, so maybe she had a hotel room. But I believe the majority was invited into our home as I slept. On Mel's days off, which were plenty during this period, she obviously had day visitors. I assume mostly Mongoloid Man, but I'll never know. Also, I suppose Mel could have arranged multiples on certain days because numbers three and four at the top of the list happened on the same day. So it's entirely possible for two males at one time. Maybe random dude three and four, or maybe random dude one came back and brought random dude five with him? Maybe both.

APRIL 2021

I was left with this constant ache that burned in my chest. I loved her with everything that I had, yet it still wasn't enough. Even after everything she had done, I was foolishly ready to give her a second chance.

I just wanted her to do the right thing. I wanted peace of mind. These were our last days together and I wanted to make them good. I wanted to feel better. I could only hope that she wanted the same.

Mel still continued her charade. She simply wouldn't give me closure. Why would she? She didn't give it to save our relationship, why would she give it now?

Perhaps I didn't know all of it, but I knew enough. We had been together for a long time and I knew her. Her actions before, during, and after, along with her reaction—the child-like lies along with the extreme guilt on her face were easy to see. I waited for her to come clean, show remorse and prove her love for me—that was all that she had to do, but never did. Instead of doing so, she would get mad and gaslight me, which she continued to do.

I couldn't make her love me. I had given her everything that I was, and it wasn't enough. It wasn't what she did that hurt the most —it was the dishonesty. That was what was eating me from the inside out. She was losing a man that loved her unconditionally, and she didn't even care.

We could have had a great life, but now I was going to have that great life with someone else. I could only wish her good luck with whatever toxic dick she ended up with.

I could barely look at her. I had lost my family and my life, and it was hard to control the emotions that roamed through me. I was terrified.

NINE
REVELATIONS OF THE PAST (MAY 2021-JUNE 2021)

ONE OF THE things I remembered was during our morning kiss goodbye, before leaving for work, Mel would quickly stick her tongue in my mouth. I thought she was joking, so I would say eww, but then she would ask if I tasted anything. I thought it was weird of her to ask me that, but I figured she was just fucking with me. Realizing what her true intentions were, made me physically ill. There were a few other times she had done this, and unfortunately for me, one of those times was when we left the lie detector. As we drove through the parking lot, Mel re-applied her lipstick and demanded I kiss her. I said no, but she kept insisting, so I leaned in for a quick peck, and she quickly stuck her tongue in my mouth, and I said eww. Again, thinking she was joking with me. But again, she asked if I tasted anything different. I didn't know what to think. I was in shock already. I played right into her game and told her I wasn't sure. I didn't believe it was a possibility that she would do that, nor would a professional lie detector guy. Then again, Mel was a petite cute girl with large breasts, and most people don't do the right thing. I don't know what happened during the lie detector test, but whatever it was, the end result was in her mouth. I drove over three hours and paid a guy five hundred dollars to have sex with my fiancé while I waited in the car. I couldn't believe it. How could this happen? Are these places set up for this type of thing? Maybe that explains the good reviews. FML. That was absolutely the worst feeling ever. That level of morality should be a crime.

Then I remembered seeing a text exchange with her slutty friend Carrie. Carrie said, "You must love Matt," and Mel replied, "I love torture, hahaha."

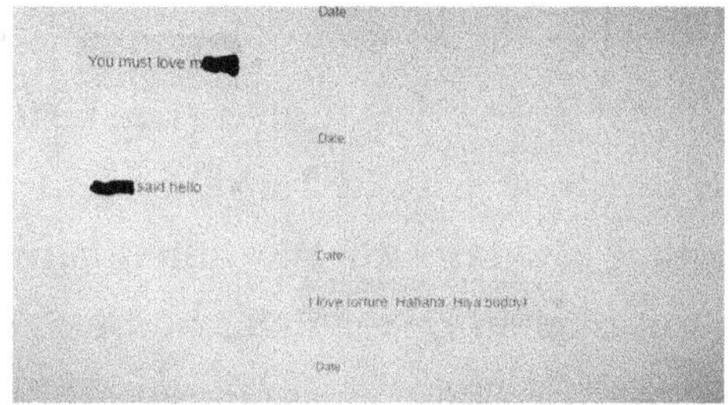

When I first saw it, I thought she was joking. Now, not in the least. She actually did love torturing me. I also didn't see any prior context for Carrie's text, which told me I was a running joke between the two for who knows how long. Our entire relationship was a farce and designed to torture me. She stayed with me for years and built a house, a farm, and a life together, just to get off on torturing me. How could anyone do that to someone? Mel once asked me what I thought about Carrie, and I told her she was ok, but I wasn't attracted to her. I think she was testing me, and I failed. Mel had previously informed me that Carrie loves unicorns; now, I finally understood what she meant. Mel was the proverbial unicorn.

There were also some texts from Steve that were strange as well. In one, Mel told Steve she was coming over, and he replied, "Sex again?" then she said, "Gimme dat bootay." In another, Mel asked for Christmas ideas, and Steve answered with a picture of a pink dildo and said it doesn't have to be pink. Mel replied with "omg," so Steve asked if she approved, and she replied with "hahaha, of course." Funny? Maybe, but with Mel's issues, not to me. I could no longer look at Mel. Her physical presence made me sick. I worried things would escalate, and something bad would happen, so I told Mel I wanted her out of the house. She said she would go to her sister's that weekend to shut me up. We argued often, but it never got physical. I never touched her or her things. Other than a few short shouting matches throughout the day, we ignored each other. I had some work in the pole barn, so I was out there all day Saturday and Sunday. Her desk and computer were gone when I returned to the house on Sunday evening. I assumed she started to move things and was relieved. But then I looked around and saw that she had just moved her office upstairs to the other bedroom. Mel didn't want to leave for some reason. Her sister had two empty bedrooms, so I didn't understand. Maybe Kelly knew and didn't want her staying there, or Mel just wanted to torture me as long as possible? Maybe both.

Then, one day, I remembered who told me to "watch her sleep." Those three words haunted me for over a year. Someone else knew, but I could never recall the memory. And finally, it popped in my head, and omg, it was her dad. Gary told me when I asked for his permission to marry Mel. After getting his blessing, this was the rest of the conversation:

Gary: you do know she is bipolar, right?

Me: no, but if she is, she hides it well. I briefly dated a girl in the past who was bipolar, and it was very evident with her. I didn't see any issues with Mel. That's when he said, "Watch her sleep." I was like, what? He said she did things at night and made some motions with his hands around his waist area. I was still like, what? (I'm slow to pick up on things) Then he just quietly blurted it out, she masturbates!

Me: (now very uncomfortable), that is just natural, and who doesn't do it? Gary replied that it was a lot and excessive.

Me: (still very uncomfortable) I never noticed; I fall asleep within five or ten minutes and sleep like a rock all night.

At that point, I just wanted the conversation to end, and I think someone had walked into the room, so that was it. I immediately decided to forget that part of the conversation, and I did forget it until that day. I had no idea the extent of what he was trying to explain to me. I wish he could have spelled it out a little more, but it's obviously been many years since Mel moved out of the family home. After remembering this, I decided to tell Mel, who told me to "watch her sleep." Not that it would change anything between us. I just wanted her to know and see her reaction. Figuring things out was my way of winning over her massive lies and betrayal. I told her it was her dad and proceeded to tell her what he had told me. Mel just shrugged it off, "What does he know? He doesn't know anything," her speech broken as her mind scrambled for another lie. I could tell she was angry that her dad told me and couldn't cover for this. She didn't say anything else and retreated upstairs. I realized this wasn't a new experience for Mel; she has always been like this. She purposely started doing things in bed before I fell asleep so that I would notice. Mel wanted me to find out.

Knowing that Mel has always been like this, I wondered what else happened in our past. When we were first together in the old house, I had my cousin Jim and some friends come over to help replace the pole barn roof. The guys would normally stay the night because of the long drive. I didn't mind because I was getting help and trusted everyone. Next was work in another barn. This time my cousin said I didn't have to pay him. Hmm, I wonder why? I guess the level of betrayal in my life runs deep. After that last job was done, we had a fourth of July party. My cousin Jim was there and drunk (along with many others). Towards the end of the night, Mel told me Jim was bothering her and hitting on her. She wanted me to kick him out. I thought he was just being a drunk idiot. We had a quick chat, and his ride took him home. No issues. Jim was probably a one-and-done to Mel. Because after a few drinks, Jim must have wanted another go, but Mel wanted nothing to do with him anymore. Besides, Mel had her eye on another friend of mine that night, Greg.

I remember waking up in the middle of the night badly needing to use the bathroom, which always seems to happen whenever I drank the night before. As I rushed downstairs, Mel was heading upstairs, quickly passing me. I mumbled bathroom, and she said she just used it, and it was open. Afterward, I walked into the kitchen, and Greg came in from outside, all sweaty and out of breath. He said he sometimes goes for a jog in the middle of the night because of Alcohol sweats or something stupid like that. He had a worried look as he made excuses to support his claim. I was still drunk, groggy, and didn't know any better and was like, whatever, and went back to bed. I bet as soon as I went back to sleep, Mel went downstairs again and finished. I realize now that is the definition of willful ignorance, and I hate myself for it. When I told Mel about it, she, of course, denied anything happening but added that Jim kissed her that night. Mel never told me that part, but it just reinforced my theories. Another time during hunting season, Greg and another friend Tom and his son, came over to hunt. Greg claimed not to feel good Sunday morning and stayed in the house with Mel while Me, Tom, and his son went out to hunt. I'm guessing they feared getting caught with Tom and his kid there during the night. It is clear to me now, at least in fragments. I wondered who else stayed over and betrayed me.

Past events where friends and co-workers acted weird in front of Mel made sense. They would either stare at her or avoid eye contact and act very uncomfortable. I asked Mel to at least tell me, "All who I know." But she continued to deny everything and told me nothing. She just continued to gaslight me. I'm delusional, the weed has gotten to my brain, and I needed professional help. Ugh, I was beyond tired of hearing that bullshit on repeat. I decided to have a small private party and invited everyone who stayed the night at the house. For some reason, I thought if I told them how Mel really was, many were involved, and it wasn't about them; maybe they would say something. If they didn't say anything, which I antici-pated, I should be able to tell if they were lying when confronted in person. With everything I have been through with Mel, one positive is I learned how to spot a lie easily. Actions and reactions, body language, eye contact, eye movement, and what they say and how they say it will tell me all I need to know. I couldn't have the meeting until Mel was gone, though. So, I planned it about a month in advance and noted it was very important that they showed up. I didn't disclose anything else. I assumed some would figure out what it was about and not show up.

In the meantime, I was mentally exhausted. Mel would not leave. She refused to stay with her sister and was waiting to find her own place. I tried to make life suck for her, but Mel pretended nothing bothered her. I could easily see the guilt, but she was too narcissistic to say anything. I deleted the DVR shows and turned off the cable. I played music loudly through the house, music that she hated. Sometimes, I put songs on repeat. One, in particular, was "I fucking hate you" by Godsmack. There were others too. Then I started to smoke in the house, which I hated myself, but I tried anything I could to drive her out. She still wouldn't leave. It was like she accepted what I was doing as punishment and just dealt with it. It was a hellish time. I told her I was going to write a book, and it would sell because people like to read fucked up shit. I think she laughed. I don't remember, but I do remember saying that she could write one too, but it would just be porn. She didn't say anything and retreated upstairs.

There was nothing I could do but wait for her to leave when she wanted to. I couldn't throw her out or touch anything she owned. I began thinking if she didn't go according to the deal we made and wanted to torture me longer, I would be fucked (not literally, though). So, I thought I better start an eviction process. I know it takes time, and I didn't want her there any longer than our deal. I had never had to do an eviction before, so it was all new to me. Among other things, I learned that Mel is considered my tenant by law. Plus, I guess calling her a whore repeatedly could be reported as harassing my tenant, and I could get kicked out of my own house. My first thought was that if I was forced to leave my own home, Mel would have more people over, which wasn't going to happen. I had to start keeping my mouth shut, or at least not long enough for her to record it. The next time we argued, she began recording, so I switched it up and started saying the names on the list. She quickly stopped and went back upstairs. She got halfway up the stairs, and I called out a name, then said otherwise known as Mongoloid Man. Mel turned and gave me an evil look. She hated that I knew. I thought good; anything that makes her regret or feel guilt works for me. Besides a few short shouting matches per day, we ignored each other as much as possible. It was extremely tense living conditions.

One day my daughter Lizzy and a friend of hers came over for a visit. Lizzy never liked Mel and knew a little of what was happening, so I didn't know what to expect. But I wasn't going to deny seeing my daughter. I think Lizzy wanted the opportunity to look right at Mel and tell her to fuck off before she was gone. Who am I to not allow her that opportunity? Mel deserved it and more. When they came over, we ate and had a good time until Mel eventually came downstairs. They exchanged evil looks and started taking jabs at each other. I enjoyed it but kept things from getting too ugly. A few minutes later, Mel went back upstairs, and we changed the subject and continued talking. I remember Lizzy asking me if I ever get in trouble at work and if my boss yells at me. I told her it's pretty rare, and it was because I always took responsibility for anything I fucked up. If something I worked on failed, I wouldn't try to blame other people or make excuses. I would stand up, admit my fault, apologize for the mistake, and then find the best solution. It's called doing the right thing, and not many people do that anymore. When I finished talking, I heard Mel sobbing upstairs. I didn't realize what I said until I heard Mel crying. I thought good; she overheard what I said. The rest of the visit went well. We spent some time outside and kept our distance from Mel.

Mel finally bought a house, but her moving day was a few days after our agreed date. I didn't say anything. I was glad she was going, and because it was after the agreed date, she would no longer get the ring or the mattress she demanded. I don't know exactly where she moved, nor do I want to know. I knew it was close to her sister, who was about an hour away, so I knew to avoid the area. I scheduled some time off from work to ensure things went smoothly. Then my STI test results came back. Yeah, I immediately got tested after realizing the list. I didn't have any symptoms, but I wanted to be sure. Surprisingly, everything was negative—a speckle of light in dark times. I felt relieved that I had figured things out before she left. I knew there was more, but I was content. I decided to start lifting weights and purchased some workout equipment. Heavy bag included. It felt good to release some frustration.

One day Mel decided to take her TV off the wall and bring it upstairs. I wasn't in the house at the time. I guess she dropped it, and it broke. She was mad, and I was amused. I told her I would have helped her if she had asked. That just made her angrier, which is exactly why I said it. She deserved it, though. She deserved every bit of bad luck. Karma. Then Mel told me that after she leaves, she wanted the right to come and visit her dead cats' graves. She had two cats before we met, but they died of old age while we were together. We buried them in the yard and covered them with large stones. I removed the stones. Mel called me an asshole after she noticed, and I told her there was nothing I could do to her that was even remotely close to what she did to me and to shut it. She did, but then she threw away pictures and things we bought while on vacation and other once meaningful items. I began to throw things away as well. I also got rid of the tulips Mel planted around the front of the house the fall prior. I ripped them out and ran them over with the lawn mower. Mel was angry and yelled at me, saying I couldn't touch her stuff. I informed her it was no longer her stuff after she planted them in the ground that only I now own. Mel thought for a second, realized I was right, and retreated upstairs. The next thing I know, she takes all her precious cross-stitches off the walls and hides them in her room. I chuckled to myself. Like I was going to destroy them or something. She will think of the great life she fucked up whenever she looks at them. So, no, I never touched those. I never damaged anything of hers. I changed the lock on my bedroom door to a keyed lock so she would no longer come into my room. Then I took the 9mm ammo she had. Eventually, she found out and asked why. I said because the ammo wasn't hers. I got the ammo from a friend, and good luck finding any (at the time, ammo shelves at retail stores were empty). She thought for a second and said ok. Good, no battle there. I slept with the door locked, and because I am a heavy sleeper, a 2x6 under the handle. Mel liked to watch all the crime shows, snapped, evil lives here, etc., and I could easily see her doing something like that, so until she was gone, things were potentially dangerous. I'm surprised she never tried to kill me. Mel was unstable and had threatened suicide multiple times in the past. Luckily, she had always bluffed and was just doing it to get her way. After I figured out the list, Mel no longer threatened suicide. Just my luck. Every night she invited strangers into our home while I was sleeping. I was one loud noise away from possible multiple homicides. Even though I am a heavy sleeper, I slept beside a loaded firearm. I have no idea what Mel told them about me, but they were very brave. I have thought about what would happen if I were to wake up and catch them. I think somebody would have been shot, and life would have turned into a whole different mess. Well, except for the single girl night. It would have been nice to join in on that one, but that would never happen because that was part of her torture. After having some beers one night, I went to Mel's room and told Mel that I would accept her, but she had to let me join. I knew we were over, but I thought maybe I could get some experience out of it before she left. I don't know what I was thinking. It's not me. It looked like she was thinking hard, so I told her to "sleep" on it and let me know in the morning. She said OK and nothing else. Around noon the next day, I asked Mel what her answer was, and she said (of course, you guessed it) she didn't know what I was talking about; I was delusional and needed professional help. It figures.

Around this time, I had a second round of kidney stones. Nice, what else could go wrong right now? I had one a couple of weeks prior, but it wasn't too bad. I toughed it out at home, and I guess it worked itself out. This one was worse. Mel acted like she cared and offered to take me to the hospital. I declined and spent the next 24 hours in pain before I drove myself in. They gave me some good stuff, and I was much better within a few hours. I should have gone right away, but I'm a guy. They gave me some prescriptions, which included some painkillers. Seeing an opportunity to be cruel, I jumped on it and rubbed them in Mel's face. I knew it bothered her, but she pretended to be unaffected. Just like the few other childish, spiteful things I did, it was minuscule compared to her actions.

That weekend, I had a bonfire and drank more alcohol. I vented to Mel through text, who was in the house. After a few hours, I head in and decide to approach Mel for maybe one last fuck. I head upstairs and knock on her door. She answers, and I open the door. She's on the bed and reading an addiction book. I told her the STI test came back negative, so I thanked her for that and said we should give it a last go. She thought about it but was quickly suspicious and said no. Oh well. One final rejection it is. I told her I would leave my door unlocked and either fuck me or kill me. I slept well and woke up.

Moving day came, and Mel was worried I would cause issues with the movers. She told everyone I was delusional and crazy. Not only was I respectful, but I also helped with a couple of things. The lead mover saw my wall mounts and was also a hunter, so we talked for a bit. That pissed Mel off. I told him Mel might take him and the other guys once they finish unloading at her place. I said it jokingly, but I knew otherwise. After moving day, Mel still had some stuff here and said she would take a couple more days to get the rest. I did not want her shit left here, so I agreed. She made a couple of trips, but instead of going back and forth, she would be gone for ten hours, leaving me to take care of her dogs. On the last trip, she had Kelly and Steve help with their cars, so they would get the last of the stuff and not come back. I didn't want to deal with her or Kelly and Steve, who was brainwashed by her or held her secret, so I avoided them. Either way, I'm sure they hated me. Twenty minutes later, they left with Mel beeping her horn as she drove away for the last time. I'm relieved, evil no longer lives here.

Mel contacted me a few days after she left and said she forgot a kitchen aid mixer. She told me to put it on the porch, and she would pick it up in a couple of days. I said fine and to let me know if there was anything else. She snapped back and said there wasn't anything more and to throw anything else away. The next day she texted and wanted more stuff. WTF, so I told her to tell me, "All who I know." She replied fuck you, keep everything; you need professional help (of course), and she was blocking me. I told her I hoped she burned in hell for eternity, which was my last communication with Mel.

May 2021 – June 2021

I could remember Mel asking me once to be bigger. Asking me what I would do to protect her, which was after the bodybuilder.

I had come to the realization that the screenshot list I had seen was from New Year's Eve through the month of January. Looking back, I now recalled that after me on New Year's Eve, she ran upstairs for something sexy to wear. I now understood that it was for the Mongoloid Man, whom she had met after I fell asleep. Everything fit. I didn't even know how anyone could hurt someone who loved them so much. She made me sick, and I couldn't believe that she kept an actual list with her.

The lie detector was a cheesy test, but she didn't want to take the risk, so she likely took care of that guy, too.

After all the conclusions I had made, I found myself wishing she had left me a long time ago. I couldn't comprehend why she would hurt someone who loved her so much—it was evil and heartless.

I could also remember sitting on the couch with her in early November 2019, talking about spicing up our sex life. Back at the time, I thought the conversation was heading in the right direction. I remembered mentioning something about other people, but I also remembered saying it couldn't be anyone we knew.

Mel took it upon herself to act on that by herself.

I believed the first time she almost told me was after her first time doing it, but she backed out and continued by herself. She should have been honest. In all honesty, one of the guys looked like a ten-year younger version of me.

I wanted to puke, but I also loved her more than anything and would have done anything to make her happy. She just needed to be honest.

All the little pieces now made sense. I could recall telling her to stop fantasizing about another dick while lying next to me and rejecting me. I told her to go be with the dick she clearly wanted and desired, and I was guessing that was exactly what she did.

Because of all that guilt, she needed me to leave her.

She gave me no choice… Still, I just wished I knew how this happened to us. I couldn't understand why she wouldn't tell me and at least give me some peace after all the heartache and pain that she caused me.

I just wanted her to give me the names, so I wouldn't have to ever be in the same room with them. I didn't want to live a lie with others I knew.

I deserve to know.

I offered to have an adult conversation with her and promised that it would stay between us… But of course, she couldn't even give me that.

I found it hard to believe that after looking back at years of vacation photographs, it had all been a lie. I was living one big fat lie, and I didn't even realize it. Now, it was all being deleted as if it never happened in the first place. It was absolutely heartbreaking to me.

Naturally, the lack of answers began to drive me insane. I questioned every man that I knew in my life, wondering if it was them that she slept with. Maybe it was Jeff… Or Dave. My cousin Jim. Anyone who looked at her weird like that.

I wanted her out of the house. If she was going to lie, she could have stayed at her John's house. That was where she belonged. She treated her dogs like shit anyway.

Every day, I wished I could remember what her dad had told me way back then. I suspected that it would have made all the difference. We would have probably been in a much different place right now. Right now, I could only hope that she would take the knife she had been stabbing me with her when she left.

What Mel did to me hurt worse than what she did with others. I hated saying mean and hurtful things to the person I loved more than anything—it hurt me more than it hurt her. It hurt me to treat her that way. It hurt me to feel all that resentment towards her.

I felt like I had no other choice because she hurt me so bad and continued to do so by not giving me closure. Honesty would have solved everything. She was my life partner, and I would have done anything for us.

We could have and should have grown together.

Soon, I lost myself in alcohol. It was hard to get through days—it felt as if I was going insane. I was trapped in *should haves* and *could haves,* but Mel cared about none of it. It was as if she liked to torture me—as if it got her off.

Ten years.

That was a good portion of our lives. That was the time we got to spend together, and I wished it would have been longer. I missed everything we had. I wished we could've grown together, but I was slow to learn, it seemed.

My health seemed to begin acting up from all the stress too. I was quite certain that I had another kidney stone—I was in so much physical pain, but it was nothing in comparison to the emotional one.

Mel was still staying at my house and offered to take me to urgent care, urging me to drink water, pretending as if she cared about my well-being after she used me and made me the clueless patsy.

The questions drove me insane.

Did she make fun of me with everyone she was with?

Did she think she could live life with me while sleeping upstairs and with other people?

How did she think that was going to work?

Why would she want to stay? To make it look like she had some sort of successful life?

Now that the gig was up, she wanted nothing to do with me, so none of that was going to happen. She was evil, and karma was a bitch.

All Mel could say was that her whole life had been about me. Everything she did, every decision she made was about me—or so she claimed. She reminded me that she came back to me (which I now so desperately wished wasn't the case).

She urged me to ask anyone at work, saying that they would tell me that all she did was talk about me, but none of that mattered now that our dreams were shattered.

"I hope you get the help that you need," she had the audacity to say. "Because I'll love you to the end."

Mel told me that she never thought of me the way I spoke about myself now—a patsy, clueless, and so on. She said she called me a dick, but it was only because she was hurting too. The rest, she claimed, I made up in my own head.

Gaslighting me to the very end. *Typical Mel.*

My drinking escalated even further. I just didn't want to hear the same old song and the same old dance anymore. I wanted her so desperately to share something new. Something genuine. Something to relieve this ache before she left.

At the very least, she could leave me a note of all those that I knew.

Jim? Greg? Hingle? Arnold? Who else was she with that I knew?

I ached for more communication. She knew I was slow to pick up on things, and she used it against me. What hurt the most was the fact that things could have been so different. Her family loved me, too.

I was also curious about how she pulled all of this off. I never took her for some kind of an evil mastermind, but apparently, that was exactly what she was.

In all of my drunken haze, a part of me wanted one last night together. The test results came negative, thankfully. It was one of many concerns I had, but at least my mind was eased in that aspect. I showered and shaved and left my door unlocked.

At that point, why not?

She could either fuck me or kill me. At this point, I didn't care.

The next morning, Mel began clearing out her things, and I did as well. She took everything from the junk drawer, including my HTC phone, which I wanted back. The video camera I decided she could keep.

Mel was upset that I took 'her' ring.

"Not your ring," I reminded her. "We never married."

She didn't comment on it. Instead, she notified me that she was going to keep the vacuum, along with her dresser and her nightstand. I kicked all of her shit out and told her that no one was allowed there. After all, I did keep my Norco there.

The dresser and nightstand were definitely not leaving my bedroom since I was the one that paid for them. Mel threatened she'd have the police over.

Most of her time was now spent outside my home. She left the dogs up to me to take care of. I'd let them out and feed them—it wasn't like she actually ever took care of them.

The discussion over who got to keep what was tiresome. She wanted the towels she got from Kohls, and still insisted on taking the dresser and nightstand.

"I bought you your tractor bucket teeth and the light on your tractor and yet, I'm not taking any of that back," she argued.

I wasn't splitting it up. She was basically taking the whole house. It was all I had left. Bedroom set and the office. She could take her bed nightstands in the pole barn, I decided.

Mel took the whole thing to another level, taking the paper plates, all garbage bags, everything in the junk drawer including the spare garage door openers, all laundry soap, pantry stuff...

I had a feeling she was just going to leave me with things that she didn't want.

As she prepared to leave, I listened to some of my old audio recordings and heard what I initially thought was her leaving the room to watch porn. I thought I heard a few porn noises, but now I knew those were real people and not porn.

I felt sick. I just wanted her to leave with as few problems as possible, and Mel said she would. She suspected it would take a few trips with her car to get it all sorted.

Kelly, Steve, and her came by to pick up everything else. She complained to be completely exhausted—that her back was hurting. So was my heart, but no one seemed to care. She reminded me that she didn't take any of her gardening stuff—that every gift I had ever given her, I now decided to keep.

I didn't care about any of that.

I did, however, decided that I was going to break down the rabbit enclosure. She could take it, seeing how they were no longer around anymore. Of course, Mel made that an issue too, telling me to give it to the neighbor, throw it out or sell it.

"Please, don't pretend you're being nice or fair, just because you bring some of my stuff from the basement upstairs," she told me.

"Alright," I responded. "Would you prefer I put all your shit in the garage and changed the locks?" At this point, I was more than ready to do it.

I gave her the step stool and the ladder, and she left the Xbox and the shotgun. Each time she took a load, she would take ten hours, leaving me to babysit her dogs.

I was certain she was doing it on purpose.

"Well, after today, you never have to see or do anything for me ever again. Thanks for watching them. I'm doing my best," she texted me.

I wasn't the only one Mel was abandoning. She decided to find a home for Ollie too, saying he was a nuisance. I couldn't say I was surprised. As soon as things didn't go her way—as soon as there were issues and hardships, she apparently abandoned both humans and dogs.

There were only a few more things left to sort out. Mel wanted the mixer that her mom gave her, as well as the make-up bag with her stuff from underneath the sink and Thomas Kincade picture. She told me to leave them on the front porch and that she'd come to pick them up.

Now that she was gone, I asked her once again to at least give me the list of everyone that she fucked that I knew. That was the least she could do.

"Forget it," she said. "I'm free from your bullshit and accusations, and I will not be controlled anymore by you. Feel free to keep the only thing I took of my mom when she passed. I want nothing to do with you anymore. Get some professional help."

For the first time, I actually hoped she'd burn in hell for this.

TEN
AFTERMATH (JUNE 2021-PRESENT)

EVEN WITH NO closure from Mel and the house practically empty, I felt better. I slept easier with her gone, and the vibrations were gone too. Who would have thought? I changed the locks, passcodes, and passwords for everything—normal stuff. I started cleaning the house and noticed that not only was my mattress stained on her side of the bed (which was not surprising, even though there was a mattress protector), but the upstairs guest bedroom mattress was also stained. The stain upstairs was near the foot of the bed, which I thought was odd, and the metal footboard was bent inward as if someone was leaning against it. Two of the three kitchen stools had stains on them as well. I remembered seeing a picture from her phone of the kitchen entrance focused on the island stools. I had to assume the worst because that's what more than likely happened. I got rid of both mattresses and all bedding and stools. After dealing with the obvious, I found an old handheld blacklight bought years ago to look for cat urine in the old house. I bought new batteries for it and hesitantly proceeded to look around. Because of pet accidents, I couldn't blame Mel for the stains on the carpet, but it looked worse than I thought and will have to be replaced. I saw suspicious stains here and there, but there was a lot of glowing stuff in the spare bedroom upstairs. It looked like someone smeared bodily fluids on the wall next to the bed with their fingers a few dozen times. Thankfully, I checked after throwing out the mattresses, upstairs frame, and bedding. But my mind still wanders; I am my own worst enemy now. It helps that I never remember my dreams at night, but daydreams have turned into nightmares. Maybe I shouldn't have looked, but at least it's clean now.

I ended up selling the shotgun and painting she left, but I didn't get much for them. No amount of money will ever make up for what she did. Nothing will. I also contacted a charity and donated a bunch of stuff she left. She left a lot because the moving truck was by weight and it was full. I either donated, burned, or threw out a lot of stuff. The house was practically empty and echoed. That brought me down quickly. I picked out and ordered new furniture, but it took almost a year to get it all because of the pandemic and shipping issues. My Mustang was running, so I was able to take that out on some joyrides and a few car shows. It needs some safety updates before I take it back to the dragstip, but anytime I drive it, it certainly takes my mind off everything else. It's therapy that works for me. I also continued to work out and dated a couple of times but was quickly discouraged. Dating is slow in rural areas as there are considerably fewer options. Sounds logical, but Mel didn't have any issues. She probably had fifty guys and a handful of girls to choose from within a week and over a few months; who knows? Things are very different for women. I realized I wasn't ready to date and needed time, so I stopped trying. Then one day, I saw a post online from an animal rescue about a dog needing a new home. I contacted them, and they put me in contact with the current owners, and we arranged for a visit. They came over, loved it, and he came to stay the next day. They told me he was five or six years old and had been abused. I thought we could both help each other, so everything seemed perfect. They only brought over three balls and a blanket, so I asked them how long they had him, and they said around five years. Wait... five years? After that, I kept the conversation short. He is spoiled now. We go for lots of walks on the property, and I've taken him kayaking. Plus, he gets along with the barn cat, so that's a good thing. Unfortunately, of the six chickens left, half disappeared, presumably from a predator, and the rest gravitated towards the neighbors' flock. It might be another year before I get more chickens, as I'm wearing myself out with work, writing, and farm duties. The garden will have to wait as well. I might grow some other stuff, though.

It was essential that I wrote everything down as soon as possible, not only before I forgot details, but so I could stop thinking about this terrible part of my life. I completed an eight-page summary and sent it to Mel's dad, sister, and her slutty friend Carrie. I wanted them to hear my side of the story. Maybe they could try to help Mel or at least do a better job of warning the next guy. Gary tried, but it wasn't clear to me, and it certainly wasn't everything. Maybe he didn't know the extent of it. He does now.

I made a final appointment with Walter. I wanted him to know that I had figured everything out, or at least as much as I could handle finding out. I read him the eight-page summary, which left him speechless and with a blank stare. I thought maybe he didn't believe me. The last time I saw him was when Mel and I picked up the lie detector results. Then I asked if he's ever heard anything like this or even remotely close to it and he said, no, nothing. I told him I planned to write a book, and he quickly agreed. I felt that if your job is to hear fucked up shit all day and have been doing it for over thirty years and never heard anything like this, it should make for a good story.

The day of the private meeting is approaching. In the days

leading up to the meeting, my cousin Jim suddenly gets sick. He messaged me and just started rambling on with excuses and unrelated small talk. His squirming made it painfully obvious. I gave him a couple of months and many chances to come clean, which he did not. I will not tolerate weak, backstabbing people, so he was blocked and out of my life. He knows that I know and will have to live with it. Everyone involved showed little guilt as long as I never found out. Now that I know, the remorse can set in, and I'm ok with that.

Next was Arnold, a guy I had known for maybe 15 years. Arnold and his now ex-wife, Heather, rented the house next to me before I moved to the farm. They were there when I flash burned my face. Arnold gave me my first tattoo in exchange for money he owed me, and we went on our first bear hunting trip together. It was unsuccessful, but it was still fun. Arnold started giving me excuses and rambling small talk as well. At first, I didn't think anything of it, but he continued, and then it clicked. Ugh, Arnold too. Come to think of it, Heather may have been involved as well. When we were neighbors, we had some drinks one evening, and Heather wanted to feel Mel's breasts. I thought it was hot, so I had no issues with it. I will never know what Mel did after I went to sleep. Heather was flirty with everyone. I recall when Arnold wasn't around, and his girl needed a ride somewhere. I agreed, and she wanted to give me road head while driving. They lived next door, and I was friends with Arnold, so I was like, no thanks. Heather would always grab my ass right in front of Arnold as well. I could see he was embarrassed. Eventually, he got tired of her behavior, and they split up a few years later. There was also a more recent time when Arnold and a couple of his friends came by to help us move our stuff into storage. The next day Mel claimed her sleeping pills were missing and accused Arnold and his friends of taking them. I asked Arnold, but he denied it and defended his friends. By now, I had figured out that whoever Mel had a one-and-done with and didn't want to deal with anymore, she would distance herself from them. She would make stories up to keep me away from them as well.

Next was my boss. He didn't show up because his daughter was getting married that day. His daughter worked with us, and I worked next to her fiancé. But I didn't know about it because it was going to be a small wedding and I wasn't invited. My boss never stayed the night at our house, but I asked him to come so he could better understand what I had been through. Also, to remind him and gauge his reaction about one evening long ago at an after-work retirement party. As Mel and I were leaving and my boss and his wife were entering, we passed each other at the door, we said hi, but for some reason, Mel mentioned that my boss was her work crush. Right in front of my boss's wife and me. An awkward moment of silence followed as my boss blushed and the look on his wife's face was not a cheerful look of approval. My boss is a good family man because I've seen him recognize and avoid opportunities and temptation. Now, if he ever stayed the night at my place to hunt (which he did not), I believe he would have been approached.

Next is Greg, whom I've known for about thirty years. I hunted with Greg often before I bought the farm. I guided him for his first successful Turkey hunt on some good property I had leased about twenty years ago. He started having kids late in life, so we didn't hunt together much anymore. He did come by a few times to hunt, a couple of times to help do some work, and to the fourth of July parties. Most of the time, he would stay the night over. He was the one I almost caught who claimed he went for jogs in the middle of the night. He didn't respond to the invitation and didn't show up, and I know why. I blocked him that night, but weeks later, I noticed in my blocked texts he sent me a text the day after the meeting, giving me some bullshit excuse of why he didn't make it. I never responded. I talked to a couple of guys who were friends with Greg as well, and they confirmed he is a piece of shit person. One of the guys suspects Greg of doing the same with his now ex-wife.

Next would be Chief, a good friend for over thirty years. He showed up and had the proper answers and reactions. I could easily see he was honest. He was jokingly upset that he wasn't approached by Mel, saying, what the hell is wrong with me? We laughed. Nothing to see here; a short paragraph for Chief.

And finally, Hingle, the last friend invited to the meeting. We've known each other since grade school, so around forty years. We were roommates a couple of times in the past. He always struggled with what he wanted to do in life and wound up doing a bit of everything. While Hingle was staying with me, he took a contract job overseas and would be gone for a year. While he was gone, I did some work on his truck, and he would tell his girlfriend, Cathy, to come over when her car needed work. Cathy came over a few times, and each time she would give me "the look" while approaching me closely. I knew what she wanted, and the answer was no. I didn't have to say it, though. It was evident in my reactions. I would never do that to one of my friends. She was super nice, just not for me.

On a side note, I talked to Cathy's sister after all this, and she told me she knew about it and Cathy definitely would have. Does everyone do this? What is wrong with people?

Hingle and Cathy later got married and then divorced shortly after. Hingle was kind of a sponge and lazy. Sort of just getting by in life. I told him to leave the last time he stayed with me. I wanted him to help work on the farm, and he started not wanting to do the "hard" jobs. We didn't talk for a while after that, but eventually ended up talking again on my yearly hunting trips and smoothed things over a little. Hingle showed up at the private party, but when he came over, he looked nervous and was anxious the whole time. We talked about other things for a while, and I had pizza delivered. After we ate, it was time to talk about what I had been through, which was the main reason for the invite. He wanted to leave, but I told him I would try to make it quick. I read Hingle and Chief the eight-page document I created. While reading, I had to turn around and yell at Hingle for playing games on his phone, not once but twice. He clearly didn't want to pay attention, and when it came time to show them the list, I don't think he even looked or cared. He just wanted to leave. The disrespect was unbelievable.

After I finished reading the document, it was time to ask Hingle if Mel ever approached him. I think he knew it was coming and wanted to talk about something else, so he asked me an unrelated question. Instead of answering his question, I asked him if Mel ever approached him. He tried to keep his head up but couldn't, he bowed his head, looked away, and quietly muttered, "She hated me." I said that wasn't what I asked, and he repeated louder, "She hated me," but eventually said no while looking down and avoiding all eye contact. If Hingle paid attention to what I read, he would have learned that Mel distanced herself from the one-and-dones. He was one of those guys who was uncomfortable around Mel, avoided her, and couldn't look at her when she was around. Hingle failed everything and was a terrible liar. He later texted me, denied anything happened with Mel, and tried to make himself a victim by saying that some girl did some shit to him. Yeah, ok. Guilt tends to dig a deeper hole.

Now I know why most of my friends didn't come over as much anymore. They acted uncomfortable around Mel, and now I know why. I remember a few of those so-called "friends" voicing their concerns when Mel came back into my life. It would have been nice if one of them bit the bullet and told me back then. Lovely world we live in. I don't know who to trust anymore. I talked to a couple of guys who worked in the shop of the company we all originally worked at and asked them if they knew anything. They denied knowing anything. The first was the top drunkard of the shop, Lenny. I thought if anyone heard late-night drunken stories, it would be him. I believe Lenny hung out a little with the drunkard grump too. I got nothing. I got the feeling that he knew something, but he didn't spill any beans. No one told me anything. Doug was the other shop guy, and one of the first times I met him, we talked by his toolbox, and he said something that stuck with me. While standing there, Mel came out of the front offices and walked through the shop. Doug noticed and started staring intensely at her as she walked across the shop. He said, "Do you know that girl?" I looked and said, "Yes, I have been seeing her for a few weeks." I don't think he heard me and certainly wasn't paying attention as he continued to stare at Mel. Then he casually said, "Yeah, she's a whore," and that he and another guy named Ray in the shop fucked her. I was shocked and again said I was dating her but louder this time. He said, "No, really?" I said, "Yes, we are dating," and he said, "oh, I was kidding." He was a joker, so I assumed he already knew we were dating and was just fucking with me. Knowing what I know now, probably not. I decided to contact him and ask him about it. It was years prior, but I thought he might tell me something now that Mel and I aren't together. So, I called him, and when I asked him about it, he said he didn't remember saying anything like that. He didn't give anything up. I always thought it was weird that Doug and Ray would always stare at Mel whenever she entered a room, even while I was talking to them. They would break eye contact with me and stare at her as she walked across the shop or office. I thought it was disrespectful, but I thought she was mine, so I didn't let it bother me. I'm not the jealous type, but I remember those occasions.

Doug actually called me out of the blue. He said he had a line on a job I may be interested in, but I told him I was taking some time off to work on a personal project. He then asked me about Mel and if I found anything more out. I thought that was strange; she had left almost a year prior. I just told him many people were involved and that I knew enough.

Doug no longer works with us, but the other guy he talked about works in the shop at my current employer along with Grump. But unlike long-term Grump, I believe the other guy was a one-and-done. Mel once told me she thought he was skinny and veiny. I don't recall the context of the conversation, but I thought it was an odd thing to say. He was thin and had visible veins in his arms, so I assumed that was what she meant. Now, maybe not so much. When I first started dating Mel, she lived in an apartment, and I remember running into this guy one day in the parking lot. He claimed his aunt or some relative lived there. What was I to think? There were many apartments around.

Another guy in the shop was obsessed with Mel—always staring and trying to talk to her. Mel complained to me about him, so I spoke to him, and as far as I know, he kept his distance afterward. I labeled him as weird but harmless. Possibly another one-and-done?

What about the neighbor, George who we got into a fight with? The argument was about a property line that neither of us had control over. Did it have something to do with Mel? George physically reminds me of Grump. They are about the same size, but George is maybe a dozen years younger. When Mel first moved in with me, we paid George to come over and let the dog out when we were at work. His wife worked, but George didn't. Perhaps there were times Mel stayed home, and he still came over? When I told George that Mel was coming back, he said, "Oh, I like Mel." I don't know what to think anymore. What about the builder or the many different contractors while the house was being built? I believe one time, Mel visited the builder at the model home by herself, and I'm sure she stayed home quite a few times while many contractors were there. Given what I know now, nothing would surprise me. For example, one day, a satellite guy came out because the internet speed wasn't usable for anything other than loading a webpage. The guy gave us the typical excuses and did nothing. Eventually, I got angry and told him to leave. Mel told me she would handle it and to go outside and calm down, which I did. If she handled it like she apparently handled everyone else, I'm sure he left happy. Those were the opportunities that I was aware of, but I'm sure there were many, many more. I will never know the true extent of her betrayal, nor do I care anymore. Some days I feel like selling everything and moving off-grid somewhere far away from people.

I was done with trying to contact people for information. No one will talk, and I can understand why. People will take this kind of stuff to their graves. So, I began gathering the information I had for the book and noticed some files were missing. I believe Mel got into my computer and deleted some items. It was not that big of a deal, as I had back-ups of most of it buried in my phone. The memory was nearly full, though, and I didn't want any more of the deleted items to disappear, so I bought a new phone. I also found some interesting information while throwing some old cards away. It was a birthday card I got for Mel. It was one of those cards that had blank areas in the text and included a bunch of word stickers you could pick from to complete the sentences. It was meant to be funny and sexy. What is interesting is some of the words she chose and that it was more than three years before this all started. I gave it to Mel, and she picked out the stickers and gave it back to me. I remember when I first read it, I laughed because of the finger and quiver line, but the last line did not make sense to me. There were much better sticker words available. It makes sense now, though, not that she had a "thingy." It read (the *italicized* word is the sticker word):

First, we could *kiss* each other's *lips*. Then I could *nibble* your *fingers* until you *quiver*. Next, you might want to massage my *body* with your hands, and I might _fondle_ your _secret place_. Lastly, we could _hold_ each other's _thingy_ with our _thighs_.

During my information gathering, I learned about BDSM and the terminology. Previously I had no idea about that stuff. Now I understand why Mel bought so many Pinnapples during that time. I don't think she put them on the porch, but I remember seeing a picture on her phone that she took of one on our counter. Plus she ate a lot of them. I've heard it makes you taste better, but I never put two and two together on that. I mean, they're good and I ate them too.

Next, I ran across a comment online from a guy I worked with many years ago about writing a book. I sent him a private message looking for tips. I told him a little about what I was writing. He told me his first wife had a drug addiction, prostituted herself for drugs, and had many stories. It sounded crazy with lots of drama, but it also sounded like something that happens dozens of times daily in every major city worldwide. However, the devil is in the details. It would be his first book as well, so I didn't get any tips. We wished each other luck, and I continued writing whenever I wasn't work-ing. I scheduled a vacation in October and wrote every day instead of hunting. In fact, for the first time in thirty years, I wasn't plan-ning on hunting this season.

After losing most of my closest friends and her family that hunted, no one was hunting. Then one day, I saw a random post a wife placed for her husband in one of the online hunting groups I joined. She claimed to have a health issue, and because her husband was taking care of her, he couldn't make it to their family property which was hours away. She felt bad and was trying to find him a closer place to hunt. I decided to reach out and offer this stranger an opportunity. Initially, he came by to check it out but didn't show up to hunt for a few weeks. When he did, he told me he had already gone to his family's property and had taken a young buck. I thought it was weird but ok. After the day's hunt, he told me he saw some good bucks fighting in the morning, but it was still dark, and then nothing after that. During the conversation, he showed me another young buck and said he shot that one too. Realizing what he had just said, he told me not to worry and would use his wife's tag if he got another one. I was disappointed but didn't say anything. I can't believe people. I wanted time to think about it. The next day, I told him to come and pick up his stuff. I previously vaguely told him why I wasn't hunting that season, and he had no issue trying to deceive me with attempted poaching. Wow, people suck ass. A giant buck was running around back there, too—his loss.

I invited Chief over for a hunt, and he harvested a nice ten-point, which took all of an hour. His biggest buck in approximately 30 years of hunting. He was supposed to go to work later that day, but he was way too excited to ruin his day with work. Being able to share what I work hard for makes everything worth it. He'll never forget that hunt. I decided to hunt in November but never had the giant buck in range, then he disappeared. I already had some venison in the freezer, so I wasn't pressured to shoot anything. I typically would hunt all day in the cushy tower blind I built when I bought the farm. I have other blinds, but this one has the best views. One day, I viewed lots of wildlife for almost the entire day. It is a special property—a hunter's dream. Towards the end of the season, my friend Tom asked to bring his 10-year-old stepson Devin out for his first hunt. "Of course!" I said. They were out for about an hour, and the kid was able to harvest a couple of does. Devin was beyond ecstatic, but the pleasure was mine as well. To be able to give someone a memory that lasts a lifetime is truly a blessing. I needed that.

A couple of days later, and it's Christmas. I spent some time with my parents and kids, which is always nice. But home remained dark and quiet. No tree, stocking, or decorations. Maybe next year. I used my remaining vacation time from Christmas to the new year to write. While working, my uncle contacted me with only days remaining in the hunting season and said he was having a hard time seeing any deer on his lease and asked if he could come out for a hunt. He is my cousin Jim's dad, but I couldn't hold that against him. He didn't know what was happening, and I wasn't going to tell him. I said, "Sure, no problem." He came out the second to the last day, and I told him where to go. I heard him shoot not long after, then another shot. He texted me and said he shot at a doe but wasn't sure if he got it and asked for help. So, I head out in the UTV, but I don't see him. I drove around, and a few minutes later, I found him. Apparently, he walked right by where I told him to go and ended up in another blind. That's ok because ten minutes after he sat down, a bunch of deer came by, and he picked one out and shot. He missed, but they didn't go far, so he picked another one out, tried again, and missed again. We looked around but didn't see anything. He then told me his shotgun was only bore-sighted. Sigh, he should know better. I offered my gear for him to use, but he declined. He came back the next day (the last day) with a different gun which he claimed to trust, but the weather was terrible with high winds and sideways snow. The deer weren't moving. Nothing was moving. It was also a toss-up on which blind to pick because we walked around a little the day before. With just a few minutes of light left, I saw some deer from the house (figures), but nothing moved where he was—tag soup for him. Not my fault, though; he should have had one in the first ten minutes.

I stayed in for New Year's Eve and was chatting with a woman I randomly met on Facebook a couple of weeks prior. We never hooked up, though. She seemed nice and was a hunter, but I think she liked the biker type. Either that or she expected me to compete with other guys for her attention, and that's not me. I wasn't ready anyway. My work kept bugging me to start coming to work again.

The requests became more frequent. I knew I had to tell them something, so I decided to explain what had happened. I couldn't just say I'm not coming in anymore. I felt I had to give them a reason, or I would get fired, so I emailed the two owners and my boss, explaining everything. They didn't reply, so I continued doing my best working from home. I used weekends and vacation time to write and research. I started in the fall and made some decent progress by the new year. The new year brought renewed vacation time, so I told my boss I wanted to take two weeks before spring. Then I took a break from writing, waiting for the vacation time to get going again. But time passes, and spring is approaching fast. I didn't get the okay for any time off yet, and they were again hassling me about coming in. I reminded them that I asked for time off at the beginning of January. I sent a vacation approval form in but did not receive anything back. I had the feeling they were not going to approve it. They wanted to force me back. Tim told me that I could pick out my own office in another building they had just acquired so I could avoid certain people. It seemed like a nice gesture, but I wasn't ready and unsure if I would ever be. I don't think I can go back to that company, at least not physically. I felt like they made their choice. I will either start my own remote business or work for another company (but mostly remote). How was I supposed to move forward in life if I worked with people who knew all this about me, let alone avoid the guys I knew were involved? What about the people I don't know? I'm sure there are more, probably many more. Every day I would be reminded of it. I would never be able to get away from it. They didn't care about the mental torture I would continue to endure. I have had more than my share of that, so I turned in my two-week notice. They claimed to understand, and I left on good terms.

During one of my self-edits, I did more research on Mel's internal "squirting" ability. I wanted to know what it was and where it came from, but previous searches yielded nothing. I thought Mel couldn't be the only one who could do it, and something would be out there. Perhaps more women could do this, but because Mel spent half her life with her hand up there, I thought she might have figured some secret female thing out. But instead of searching for sexually related abilities, I looked into medically related reasons and found something that logically explained Mel's ability. Vesicovaginal Fistula (VVF) is an abnormal opening between the bladder and vaginal cavity. I wouldn't have included it if she didn't use it as a sexual tool. She may have purposely used a needle or something and did that to herself the night before showing me. Her VVF must have been small because it took me "blocking" the normal path and her squeezing her bladder internally. That means it's urine like porn shows, just coming out of another hole. Finding this out triggered a memory of an odd conversation we had when Mel told me urine comes out of the vagina. I told her no, it comes out of the urethra, the small hole just above the fuck hole. Surprisingly she disagreed and was serious about it. I didn't want to argue about her body, so I just told her to google some images. Now I think about it; maybe she didn't know because the typical causes of VVF are pregnancy, surgical trauma, and preadolescent trauma. As far as I know, Mel never had children, but surgical trauma she kept to herself is a possibility. Mel had many secrets. But what Mel told me about her urine led me to believe something may have happened to her when she was very young. Some major symptoms include incontinence and pain during sex, which sounds logical. But being with Mel for nine years, I have never noticed any signs of incontinence. We would take half-day hikes or work outside for hours, and she never wore a pad unless it was shark week. She never smelled bad either. So, no issue there. For the pain during sex part, Mel had told me many times that sex was painful, but she never showed any signs of pain or discomfort—only pleasure. Plus, if sex caused pain, why all the partners? Not to mention the prefer-ence for mongoloid man. I don't understand most of it and never will.

So that's my fucked up story, the best I can remember. I never had solid evidence of anything. Without the list, which was only strong circumstantial, I never would have known the extent of it. Hell, if Mel never started "something different" with me, I wouldn't have known any of it. Mel found the perfect victim with me. I loved and treated her well, but most importantly, I fell asleep fast and slept hard. It was only after years of hidden abuse that she started to torture me blatantly. Even then, it took me a long time to figure out what was really happening. I was always a step or two behind. I didn't have the experience to recognize the red flags and make sense of some observations, but sadly, now I do. Willfully ignorant and blissfully ignorant, yes, I was, and both could make decent titles, but I'm Sleeping covers that and more.

Would I have been better off not knowing? If I decided to leave Mel before I figured everything out? I thought it was only Grump until the very end, so I would still be hanging out with the other backstabbing liars and their secrets, individually laughing behind my back. I'm pretty sure they didn't know about each other, so each one probably thought they were special. But I wouldn't have known; I'd still be sleeping. But now that I woke up, I confess there are parts of me that are jealous. The same parts that fantasize about this stuff but never act on them. Maybe because I never had an opportunity, but more than likely, I did and didn't see it. Do I think it would have worked out differently if I were more observant and known from the start? For sure, because none of this shit would've ever happened. It's depressing to think about. Now, daydreams of a zombie apocalypse or a national purge day make me smile. But until that happens, I will continue to pick up the pieces and patch together what I can.